Congratula...
I hope you enjoy
MzSassy

Allured

A Turner Family Novel

MzSassytheAuthor

Allured

Contact the Author:
mzsassytheauthor@gmail.com
Instagram: mzsassytheauthor
Facebook.com/mzsassytheauthor
Twitter: mzsassytheauth1

Book and Cover design by:
Amethyst Phoenix Press

First Edition: August 2021
ISBN: 978-1-7369722-2-9

Prologue

Anastazia Rose Turner parked her Volkswagen Beetle in front of the three-story brownstone and cut the engine off. Sighing lightly, she reached into her passenger seat and picked up her over-the-shoulder bag that held her notepads, journals, and favorite writing pens. Opening up her car door, she inhaled the light breeze that always seemed to bring a sense of enjoyment, marking the beginning of summer. Locking her doors and making her way around the front of her car, she stepped onto the walkway leading to the brownstone with the most elevating sense of excitement. This was going to be the best summer of her life; she just knew it. She decided to take a journalism class over the summer, another lesson to add to her long list of others as extra course credits for college. She wanted to be a writer or journalist or maybe an author. Honestly, she wasn't sure yet. She knew no matter what she decided; she would receive significant support from her family.

Finally making it up the steps, she rang the doorbell with jittery nerves. She wasn't nervous about the interview she was conducting with the couple chosen first; she was excited about the outcome. Her assignment was to write about something she was passionate about, something anyone could relate to, and something anyone could enjoy. Anastazia chose love. But not just any love, the love she'd grown up watching unfold before her very eyes. It was no secret that she was the daughter of Boston's well-known and prominent attorney James Turner, nor was the love story surrounding her parents any secret. Boston's elite were all well-versed in the teenager couple that had fallen in love, married at the age of 18, and still were going strong. Of course, she wasn't there to witness the marital bliss of her parents or grandparents for that matter; however, she had seen the love finding, joining, and binding of each of her uncles and aunt. Her father had three brothers and was the third son of Justin and Nancy Turner Sr. Her aunt, her mother's younger sister, had also gotten married within the last year. She'd had the pleasure of witnessing all of their joyous unions. Of course, being much younger for some of them, she didn't fully understand what was going on. She just knew that she was able to wear a pretty dress, toss flowers down the aisle and see her grandmother shed happy tears.

The door to the brownstone opened, and Anastazia was greeted in the most loveable way.

"Stazia girl." Her uncle Jacen belted while pulling her in for a hug.

"Hi, Uncle Jacen!" She said as he hugged her tightly.

"Look at you trying to grow up and driving, I see." He nodded his head toward her deep-sea teal beetle. Pulling back, she smiled up at him.

"Yes, dad finally caved." She said, showing very little guilt in knowing her dad wanted her to wait another year before getting her a car. Her mother had helped in persuading him. James Turner was not easily won over as a lawyer, but his one weakness was his wife. There was absolutely nothing James Tuner wouldn't do for his wife of twenty years.

"What's that on the headlights?" Jacen asked. Anastazia looked over to see what he was talking about and did her best not to laugh.

"Lashes. Compliments of auntie Kaitlyn." she said proudly.

"Why am I not surprised? Only Kaitlyn would think to put lashes on a car." He responded, shaking his head and inviting her inside. It was her first time in the brownstone, owned by her newest aunt Chelsea. Although, her family considered Chelsea's family long before she'd married her uncle Jacen last year. Chelsea had been an intern at the magazine agency her aunt Shayna worked for. Anastazia adjusted her bag, which had slightly slouched from her shoulder due to her uncle's smoldering hug. She walked inside the brownstone, loving the open and airy essence of the first floor.

"Chelsea will be down in a minute." her uncle told her while offering her something to drink. She decided on a Mountain Dew and placed her bag on the island's chairs.

"So, what's this project you're doing that everyone has been talking about." She tried to hide her smile as she accepted the glass with her drink of choice in it.

"It's going to be a collection of love stories, so to speak." she answered. She wasn't sure how it would all turn out, but she looked forward to the project.

"And you figured why not start with family?"

"Yes. My family is blessed with many happily ever after's." she boasted while smiling ear to ear. She was almost coming out of her skin with excitement.

"Yes, I think we are blessed in that way." He didn't finish his statements as they both turned at the light footsteps coming down the stairs. Anastazia turned to see Chelsea approaching them. She looked comfortable in a pair of loose black shorts, an oversized t-shirt she was sure belonged to her uncle, barefoot, and her sandy red hair in a messy bun.

"Hey, Anastazia." Chelsea said while opening her arms for a hug. Anastazia went willingly, loving the happiness showing on her new aunt's face.

"How are you doing?" Anastazia asked, engulfed in the hug and feeling the slightly protruding belly under the massive shirt. It wasn't too long after her aunt returned from a trip to Houston that she announced she was pregnant. Pulling back, Anastazia could see what others referred to as a pregnancy glow on her aunt's face. The baby was said to be due late this summer or early fall. According to her grandmother, Chelsea seemed to carry the baby in her back because she wasn't huge in the front.

"I'm so happy you included us in your project." Chelsea said.

"Hey, I figured there were no better stories about love than in my own family." Anastazia said as she took a seat on the island chair next to her bag. Chelsea walked over to Jacen, who naturally opened his arms to her and kissed her head as she snuggled into him.

"Well. I'm ready to get started if you are." Jacen stated.

"Alright." Anastazia reached over to grab her notepad and pens.

"Did you want to stay in here or sit in the living area?

"Here is fine." Chelsea answered. Anastazia nodded and grabbed her journal and pen from her bag. She also set up the recorder on her phone.

"So, where do you want to start?" Anastazia asked, ready to record and write her notes. Jacen looked at his wife, allowing her to decide.

"I think we should start from the favor." Chelsea answered, smiling.

Chapter One

Jacen threw on his shirt after hearing his phone ping again with what he was sure was another fifty-line text message from Lauren. Did women think guys read all that? He ignored it, heading to the bathroom to finish getting ready. He was sure Lauren was still in a rant about their breakup, if you could call it that. Since Trent got married, making Jacen Boston's most eligible bachelor, women had been on the prowl. He and Lauren had been on three dates before Trent's wedding, and afterward, she just assumed she was the next lucky lady. Going so far as to contact his mother for her opinion on wedding colors. That ended whatever she thought they had going on. He didn't have any problems with marriage. His parents had been married for more than forty years. All of his brothers were married, and now both of his best friends were married. All of them were lucky enough to find brilliant and beautiful women. His problem wasn't finding good women, he believed they were out there, and women came easy to him, but where was the one tailor-made just for him. He wouldn't call himself a romantic, but he did believe in soulmates, partners, best friends. His dad would tell him about his mom, that she was his best friend, the one he couldn't live without. The closest Jacen could recall to a best friend that was a girl, was Kaitlyn, who just married his best friend Trent and was the younger sister of his brother James's wife, Kaycee.

He and Kaitlyn had been two peas in a pod. Because Kaycee and Kaitlyn's dad was strict when it came to dating, James and Kaycee had many dates under the watchful eye of their parents and his. Thrusting him and Kaitlyn, as the younger siblings, together a lot. That was cool with Jacen, Kaitlyn wasn't a regular girl. She was a tomboy through and through. Doing any and everything not to be the girly girl lady her mom insisted on her becoming. But that was then, and now she was utterly in love with Trent. They were married now, working on baby number two. Jacen's cell phone pinged again, and he blew out a slow breath and went to his nightstand to retrieve it, praying it wasn't Lauren. He felt relief when he saw it from Chelsea, confirming everything was going well at the club. He texted back thanks and finished getting ready.

Chelsea placed her phone in her back pocket after seeing Jacen's response. It was another typical afternoon, and Chelsea was cleaning down tables and chairs at Jacen's club. Call her crazy but cleaning always seems to help clear her mind, and today she needed it more than ever. After finishing editing another wonderful romance novel in the making, she took a quick shower and headed to the club. The damper in her day was the invitation to her sister's wedding. The invitation sent an unsettling feeling inside of her. Chelsea wondered if she'd gotten it by mistake. She wasn't on good terms with her sisters and hadn't been for years.

"Hey Chels, did the new shipment of glasses come in?" The bartender, Josh, asked, interrupting her thoughts.

"Yes, they're back on the third shelf."

"Thanks. I want to have those put out before the boss gets in." Chelsea smiled, and Josh headed to the storage room. She was proud of him, he didn't come from the best background growing up, but he was attending Boston University after two years at the local community college studying to be an engineer. He started working for Jacen a few weeks before Chelsea did or before she began to help out. She laughed to herself, remembering how it all went down.

Chelsea and Ashiree were drinking champagne and laughing at a few jokes with some football players on the team with Trent. Chelsea decided to take a quick bathroom break, and after she finished and walked out of the bathroom, she saw Jacen at the end of a hall on his phone. He seemed so distressed. Not wanting to be nosey but also concerned with the stress etched over his face, she walked over to him.

"I'll be there shortly." She heard him say before disconnecting the call.

"Is everything okay?" Chelsea asked. He turned toward her and rubbed his hand down his face.

"I have an issue at Ensconce. A fight broke out, and two of my servers are hurt. The police are already there, and an ambulance is on its way."

"Are the police closing the club?"

"Not according to Evan, but I might have to. I'm down two servers."

"I can help." She offered immediately.

"I can't ask you to do that." Jacen said.

"Not ask her to do what?" Ashiree asked, approaching them in the hall.

"Jacen has an issue at the club, he's down two servers, so I'm volunteering. We both should.' Chelsea suggested.

"I love the way you're just volunteering my services." Ashiree said.

"It's okay, Ashiree. I can manage. I need to tell Trent I'm leaving." Jacen said grudgingly.

"Are you really in a bind?" Ashiree asked with genuine concern.

"Yes." Jacen admitted.

"Well, Trent and Kaitlyn are about to leave, so we can see them off and then head to the club."

"Are you going to help?" Jacen asked, mildly shocked.

"Hey, I've had my fill of flirting with football players." She answered with a shrug.

"Thanks, I truly appreciate it. I'll meet you two at the club as soon as we see the happy couple off." Chelsea and Ashiree nodded and agreed as Jacen walked off toward the hall.

"You're a lifesaver." Chelsea praised.

"Yeah, yeah. You owe me." She said with a pointed finger.

"I know, I know," Chelsea said, grabbing Ashiree's arm as they went to see the couple off.

Chelsea finished wiping down the last of the tables and looked around before making her way upstairs. She saw Heidi, the manager of the diner, talking with one of the cooks. She waited until Heidi noticed her.

"Hey, Chelsea."

"Hey Heidi, how's Sammy doing?" Chelsea asked. Sammy was Heidi's seven years old son.

"He's doing great. He wants to take karate classes." Heidi said proudly.

"I think that's great."

"I hope so. It's been kind of hard living here after Samuel passed away. My parents insist on me moving back to Charleston, but I don't want to leave. Samuel loved it here. We fell in love here. I guess I'm just not ready to let go yet." Chelsea's heart went to Heidi. She'd lost her college sweetheart less than a year ago due to his plane being shot down by the enemy while overseas.

"Well, I'm sure he will like it." Chelsea encouraged.

"Me too; it's pretty expensive." They chatted a little before Heidi did her rounds around the dining area. Heidi assured her that they didn't need any help, so Chelsea decided to head home.

~~~~~~~~~~~~~~~~~~~~~

Jacen attempted not to speed in traffic while his sister-in-law Shayna continued explaining his need to be the main attraction in the upcoming charity calendar.

"I don't understand why you're so difficult about this."

"I'm busy, Shayna. You know I'm working on a few projects to expand the club."

"But it is a Turner family tradition?"

"Just email me the dates for the photoshoots and events, and I'll see what I can do." He sighed heavily.

"I'd prefer you telling me you'd clear your schedule to ensure you are there, but I'll take what I can get for now…see you Tuesday night."

"I'll see you then." He ended the call and took a long breath. He looked forward to being in the charity calendar in his younger days, doing the photoshoot, and attending all the events that went into Boston's Calendar bachelor. The attention alone was any single man's dream. All of the proceeds from the calendar went to Boston's inner-city community centers and the Bachelors' charity of choice. Shayna sponsored the event each year. His dad and uncle had done it, all his older brothers, and his friend Trent. Over the years the calendar photos shifted to more family friendly than hot and seductive. Before Trent's wedding, he was ready, but everything changed, and he was losing his spirit to participate or more, so his focus. He got an unexpected call from a good friend of the family to consider an opportunity to expand his club.

Branding was something Jacen was seriously looking into, but the capital to back it up would require more risk than reward if not done correctly. The upcoming charity events for the calendar, would create conflicting schedules should the expansion begin. Then, of course, he needed a date. He didn't have a problem finding a date, he had his pick, but he didn't want to focus on having the right woman on his arm. He didn't want another Lauren, assuming that each date was a marker for getting to the altar. He needed a steady girl who could look the part, be gracious in understanding it was about the kids, and potentially go their separate ways afterward. Six weeks that's all he needed, six weeks. Later that evening, Donovan and Trent decided to stop by Ensconce, and they were all sitting at the bar as the crowd in the club was low.

"I don't see what the problem is; just pick a girl." Trent suggested. Jacen sighed.

"It's not that simple, and I don't have time to date and filter through for the best woman that won't get attached." Jacen said.

"Well, you can hang that up. They all get attached." Trent said.

"They don't all get attached." Donovan responded.

"Says the man my sister couldn't get unattached to since she was ten." Trent said. Donovan smiled, thinking of his beautiful wife.

"Point made."

"Look, I have a lot of things coming up with trying to expand the club. I don't have time to really date anyone."

"Why don't you just ask Chelsea?" Trent suggested. Jacen looked at him and pondered on it.

"That's not a bad idea, assuming she's not dating anyone." Donovan said.

"I doubt she is. She's at Jacen's diner practically every day. How he turned one night of help into three months, I'll never understand." Trent added.

"How did you do that exactly? " Donovan asked Jacen. He simply shrugged his shoulders.

"Well, going with the assumption she's single, do you think she'd agree to help out?" Trent asked. Jacen wasn't sure, but the more he thought about it, the more he liked the idea.

"Hey, I won't know until I ask." Jacen finally said.

Chapter Two

"You can do this, Chelsea; you can do this." Chelsea had been talking herself into asking Jacen to be her date for the wedding. It was all Ashiree's fault after finding out on social media from Lauren ranting; Jacen had called it off with her. Ashiree had been in her ear all night about how God opens doors. It was just for the weekend. He would be perfect for showing off to her family. She recalled the conversation last night.

"I'm just saying, Chels, you could hire somebody if you had to." Ashiree suggested.

"Or...you could come with me." She smiled adoringly.

"I wish I could, but I have a major project at work coming up, and I have to be focused." Chelsea sighed as she took a sip of her wine. She explained the wedding invitation to her best friend Ashiree, who was pretty shocked about it. Chelsea didn't want to go home by herself, so she asked Ashiree, and somehow that turned into a conversation about bringing an actual date, a male date.

"You work part-time at a bar, and you can't get anyone willing to spend a weekend in a mansion on top of a hill." She laughed sarcastically. The problem was most people didn't know Chelsea's past, at least not all of it. Most knew she was raised by her aunt, who passed away three years ago, left her a brownstone, and after college, she went to work for Show Stoppin magazine, where she met and worked as an assistant for Shayna Masters now Shayna Turner. Once the magazine took a turn for the worse, she worked part-time as a book editor for romance authors. She loved it, and over the last five years, she'd enjoyed doing it full time.

"Why don't you just ask Jacen?" Ashiree suggested. Chelsea gave her a side-eye.

"I'm serious. He owes for all the work you've done at the diner." Ashiree continued.

"I honestly don't mind, but no, I couldn't ask Jacen. He's dating Lauren."

"No, he's not. She's been ranting her 'woe is me post all over IG. Besides, I don't understand how anyone could date that girl."

"She's not that bad."

"You just like to see the good in people, but not focusing on Lauren; I was just thinking of the jaw drops from your sisters if you walked in with Jacen Turner's sexy self."

"And here I thought Justin was your favorite Turner brother."

"Oh, he was, but I had to stop fantasizing about him years ago."

"Oh really? And Why is that?" Chelsea asked skeptically.

"I met Alexia." Ashiree sighed, sinking further into the couch."

"She's great, isn't she?"

"Yes, and I was so prepared to hate her for stealing my man." They both shared a laugh.

Bringing her thoughts back to the present, Chelsea understood Ashiree wanted Chelsea's family to see her doing well. Still, Chelsea didn't care what her sisters thought of her, she would never receive their approval or acceptance, and she gave up wanting it a long time ago. But she didn't want to go alone, and her father practically begged her the other night to attend. Her biggest concern now was asking Jacen and hoping he wouldn't mind helping her out.

She considered them friends over the last few years and hoped he'd see it as helping a friend out. She headed to the back where his office was. He never closed his door if he was in his office. Jacen always wanted any of his staff to feel comfortable enough to walk in. His office included a lounger, a giant screen tv, and an awkward-looking cactus plant in the corner.

"Hey Jacen, can I talk to you for a second?"

"Hey Chelsea, Sure, come on in." He said. She walked into his office and took a seat in a chair in front of his desk.

"I have a favor to ask of you." she began.

"Do you? Interesting, so do I." Jacen admitted.

"A favor, really?"

"Yes. Why don't you go first?" he suggested.

"Okay, I have a wedding to go to in a couple of weeks." She began, Jacen laughed.

"Chelsea, you do realize you don't actually work for me, right? If you're going to be out of town, you don't have to tell me."

"Oh, I know, I mean, I probably would anyway, but that's not it."

"So, what is it?"

"I need a date."

"A date? To a wedding?" He asked with a quirked brow.

"Yes," she answered nervously, "and I was hoping you wouldn't mind." The initial shock on Jacen's face was quickly replaced by a huge smile that she couldn't explain.

"You are not going to believe this." he began.

"I understand if you don't want to." She interrupted, preparing herself for his rejection. "I mean, we're friends, and if it's awkward then..." she tried to explain, but he cut her off.

"Chelsea, no, it's just... well, I'm in a little of a dilemma myself that I would like you to help me out with." Jacen said, a slight edge of uncertainty in his voice.

"Oh?" she asked, wondering what his dilemma could be.

"Yeah, see..." he started, rubbing a hand down his face.

"Hey boss, we're having an issue with today's delivery. The regular guy is on vacation, and the new guy is complaining about the address being off one number." Both of them turned toward Jacen's doorway at Josh's interruption.

"Okay, here I come." he said with a sigh to Josh. Looking at Chelsea, he said. "We'll continue this conversation later, but yes, I'm sure going to the wedding will be okay." he winked at her and headed out of the office. Chelsea breathed a sigh of relief and stood. That had gone easier than she'd thought. However, her mind pondered on what dilemma he needed her help with. She decided to head home and Facetime Ashiree as soon as she walked into her brownstone.

"So he agreed?" Ashiree asked, practically dying to know the answer.

"Yes." Chelsea nodded while heading to her kitchen to grab a bottle of water.

"That's so great, well at least you can go to your sister's wedding with a little man candy on your arm." Ashiree said.

"I think there's a catch."

"Like?"

"Like he has a dilemma he wants me to help him out with." Chelsea said nervously.

"Which is what exactly?"

"I don't know. He didn't get a chance to tell me before Josh interrupted us about a delivery."

"Well, it's a bit rash, but sexual favors in exchange for being with your family isn't completely unheard of." Ashiree teased.

"Ashiree Morgan!"

"What? I'm just saying." Chelsea watched Ashiree shrug her shoulders.

"I'm not trying to have sex with Jacen Turner."

"Half the women in Boston are trying to have sex with Jacen Turner." Ashiree countered. Chelsea shook her head and took a swig from her water bottle, pondering on Ashiree's words.

"Do you think he's really going to ask me for sex?"

"No, I'm sure he doesn't have to ask for it, but I know you like Jacen."

"I do not like…" she tried to deny.

"Don't lie. You do." Ashiree said through the phone sternly.

"I'm not his type." Chelsea stated, walking over to her living area plopping down on her loveseat.

"But he's yours."

"I don't have a type. And you're one to talk." Chelsea said.

"What? I know I have a type. Give me a man with dimples, and I'm a goner."

"Like you'd ever settle down." Chelsea teased.

"Hey, I'm not the hopeless romantic like you."

"It's a hopeful romantic. Why do people say hopeless when it's what they're hoping for?"

"Beats me, but back to Jacen Turner."

"We're just friends, Ashiree." She said in an exasperated sigh.

"Okay, okay, I'll lay off." She held her hand up in surrender. "Anyway, I have a big board meeting tomorrow. Doesn't that sound fun?" She said, rolling her eyes.

"I'm sure it will be alright...night, Ree."

"Night, Chels."

~~~~~~~~~~~~~~~~~~~~~~~~

He should just call her. Things were crazy after the delivery mix-up at the club, and Jacen never got the chance to talk back with Chelsea before she left. He was pacing around his living room. Why was he nervous? This was Chelsea. Plus, she invited him to a wedding as a favor. It wasn't a problem. It was a favor for a favor. But who was he kidding? Ever since his talk with Trent and Donovan, he began to see Chelsea differently. Like the other day, for example. He was pretty sure he'd seen her in jeans before. But somehow, they seem to catch his attention. She came to the diner around two every day to help. Once finished, she would check to see if there was any help needed in the club. She was wiping down tables, Josh put on some Reggae music during the shift change, and Chelsea swayed her hips to the beat nonchalantly. He caught himself a few times staring longer than he knew appropriate. She was a friend more like family. Shayna kind of took Chelsea under her wing when she'd first started working for her. What was that six, no, eight years ago? He rubbed his hand down his face. He needed to get himself together and keep it simple. One weekend for her and Six weeks of dates for him. No longer wanting to delay the inevitable, he dialed her number. She picked up on the second ring.

"Hey, Chelsea."

"Hi, Jacen."

"I didn't wake you up, did I?"

"No. I just got off the phone with Ashiree."
Chelsea said.

"And how is she doing?"

"Fine. She has a big meeting tomorrow." He
nodded until he realized she couldn't see him. Silence
hung for a minute before he noticed he was stalling.

"We didn't get a chance to finish our
conversation earlier." Jacen said.

"Yeah, things got a little busy for you."

"So, when is this wedding?" Jacen asked.

"Two weeks from Saturday. It's a weekend
affair, but if that doesn't work. It's fine. I just need to
be there for the wedding."

"Are you in the wedding?" He asked and
heard her take a slow breath. He wondered if she had
any idea how sexy that sounded.

"No."

"Okay. I'm sure I can adjust, plus it kind of
helps me out."

"You did mention something about that."
Chelsea inquired.

"Yes, so you know the charity calendar
Shayna does every year."

"Of course. Boston Most Eligible Bachelors in the flesh...Oh my gosh, I just realized that's you this year." He inwardly groaned. Years he'd been waiting for this opportunity. To have himself plaster all over twelve months of the year for any woman to see. It seemed so shallow now.

"Yes, and I need a date or, more so, several dates." There was complete silence on the phone. He wondered for a second if the call dropped.

"Chelsea, are you there?"

"Um-hm." He had no idea how to take that response. He wished he could see her face right now. Was the thought that bad to her?

"How many dates are we talking about?" Chelsea asked.

"All of them." He answered.

"The shooting goes on for almost two months."

"Yes." He responded, knowing she knew firsthand how the process of making the calendar went.

"And you want me as your date?"

"Yes."

"For all of them?"

"Yes, Chelsea." He sounded like a broken record. He wanted to know from her tone if she was shocked or appalled by his request. Six weeks was asking a lot.

"I can find a way to compensate you. I kind of owe anyway since you come to the diner every day and help out.

"You don't have to pay me. I like helping out."

"So, what is it?"

"The only bachelors that have one woman doing the calendar are the ones with girlfriends. People will think we're dating." She nailed it on the head. That's what he wanted them to think, especially to the prowlers looking to be the next Turner wife.

"That's exactly what I want." Jacen admitted.

"You actually want people to think we're together?"

"For the next two months, yes." He really would give anything to see her face right now. To watch her expressions, getting some kind of idea of what thoughts were going through her head. But the more he thought about it, the more he liked it. Maybe Chelsea needed time to think about it. He did just spring it on her. He considered her a friend, but outside of the few times she'd come to his family gatherings or at the diner, he never really spent time with Chelsea.

"How about you take a couple of days to think about it?" Jacen suggested.

"I think I might need that." Her tone made him cautious. Did she really not want to do it? He honestly hadn't thought she would turn him down. If she were unsure or uncomfortable with it, he wouldn't pressure her.

"Just take a few days and let me know. No pressure, Chelsea. Whether you agree or not, I'll still come to the wedding."

"You will?"

"Of course." he meant it. It was the least he could do with all that she'd been willing to help him out with.

"Thank you, Jacen."

"You're welcome. Goodnight, Chelsea."

"Good night." After ending the call, he let the conversation replay in his head. To say he was disappointed was putting it mildly. Sure he could find a date to any function he had to attend, but he wanted

Chelsea to be with him. He wondered what it would take to convince her.

Chapter Three

"Wait? So he asked you to be his date for all the calendar events?"

"Yup." Chelsea said, twirling the spoon around in her hot chocolate, trying to calm the nerves in her stomach. Jacen Turner wanted her to be his fake girlfriend for the next two months. It wasn't a bad idea, considering she had every intention of using him as her fake boyfriend for her sister's upcoming nuptials. But that was different. She didn't live in the same city as her sisters, didn't have lunch with their friends, and didn't have the prowling entourage of ladies wanting to chop her head off at any moment. Okay, so maybe it was a little extreme to think someone would go that crazy.

"I don't understand why you're not leaping for joy right down. This is practically a dream come true." Ashiree said, cutting into her pancakes. They decided to have a girls' morning out for breakfast at the local IHOP.

"It's not real, Ashiree."

"It can be." She said, now pouring half a bottle of syrup over her pancakes.

"I don't know why you even get pancakes. You end up eating a plate of syrup anyway." Ashiree loaded her folk with cut pieces of her pancake dripping with syrup as she lifted it into her mouth and savored it with a moan. Chelsea rolled her eyes at her.

"I love food." She finally said after finishing her folk load and began to repeat the process. Chelsea tried not to be jealous. Ashiree could eat an elephant and never gain a pound. She, on the other hand, was probably gaining an inch by just watching Ashiree eat.

"Me and food have a love-hate relationship." Chelsea responded, finally taking a sip of her hot chocolate. Allowing Ashiree a few more forkfuls, she glanced outside the window. She watched as people walked by, gripping their coats and hats as the wind blew. Thankfully, the forecast had not predicted snow, but it was definitely heading toward a cold front.

"So back to the matter at hand." Ashiree said, wiping her hands and fingertips with a wet wipe. "I think you should accept. Enjoy every bit of Jacen's assets and have memories to last you a lifetime."

That's what she was afraid of. Having memories of him that would last a lifetime. It was one thing to dream of someone and a totally different issue to actually have moments with them.

"That's not as easy as it seems."

"What's the hard part, Chels?" She looked back into her cup. Now half empty. Then back up to Ashiree.

"Telling my heart that it's not real." She wouldn't lie to herself. She'd wanted Jacen Turner from the first time she'd seen him at Show Stoppin' magazine. The assistant editor at the time was Shayna. She showed Chelsea the ropes, taking her under her wings and explaining how to run a magazine. The stories highlighted the beauty tips that fit the current trend, and even included a section to help women understand sports better. Shayna was conducting interviews on local businesses, spotlighting success or expansion. A very handsome twenty-two-year-old Jacen Turner walked into the office. Dressed in black jeans, a long black coat, and a black cap hat. Every girl in the office stopped what they were doing to notice him. It was hard not to. At 6'4', the youngest of the Turners brothers was a sight for sore eyes. Dark mocha brown skin, deep brown penetrating eyes, full lips, and a clean-shaven face. Chelsea had been getting Shayna coffee at the time when he strolled up to her and asked if Shayna was ready for him. She'd almost dropped the cup in her hand. Completely speechless, Chelsea nodded and pointed to Shayna's office, forgetting she was supposed to bring her coffee. Finally finding her brain, she walked in after him, watching the greeting between the two of them. She sat through the entire interview, trying to focus on anything other than his presence, which was impossible. There was no ignoring Jacen when he was around. Adding to the ultra-sexy exterior, Jacen was a smart man. The interview spotlighted the diner he owned, now adding a nightclub. It wasn't a secret in the city that Jacen was given the diner he started out as a busboy in high school. After that interview, it was safe to say Chelsea had her leading man in all her nighttime fantasies from then on. But Jacen was a ladies' man; even before his brothers were married, women flocked to him. Seeing the women he was dating and noticing their similarities, it was safe to say she wasn't his type. Shayna practically considered her family now, and she attended several functions with the Turner family and their friends.

"Earth to Chelsea," Ashiree said, waving her hand and bringing her out of her thoughts. "Did you hear a single thing I said?" She was almost embarrassed to say she hadn't.

"I'm sorry, what did you say?" Ashiree quirked a brow at her, annoyed Chelsea hadn't been listening.

"I was suggesting we hit the pool hall sometime this week." She repeated.

"Oh, that's fine." Chelsea agreed, smiling and casting her worries aside, at least for now.

~~~~~~~~~~~~~~~~~~~~~~~~~

"Jacen, are you listening to me?" Jacen popped his head up from looking at his phone. He honestly hadn't been listening. Another investor he hoped to partner with just declined his offer.

"Sorry, Shayna." He said, putting his phone back in his pocket. She narrowed her eyes at him. Placing her hands entirely on her desk and intertwining her fingers.

"I was asking you about social functions we plan for you to make an appearance at and which ones you will have a date for."

"I'm not sure yet." He answered honestly. Two whole days and no word from Chelsea.

"I'll need you to get that information to me as soon as possible. We have special preparations we'll have to make in shooting with your dates." He nodded but didn't reply. He honestly didn't like the assumption she made that he would have more than one date. Shayna continued giving him a rundown over the next six weeks' events and eventually handing him an itinerary.

"I'll let you know by the end of the week. Thanks, Shayna." He said, standing and began to leave her office.

"Jacen." She said in a firm voice. He turned to see her standing behind her desk.

"Yes."

"You don't seem as excited about this as I assumed you would be."

"No, I am. It's a lot of things happening at once. That's all, I promise." She nodded, but he could tell she wanted to pry for more information. Shayna was the nosiest of all of his sisters-in-law, and she wasn't ashamed of it.

"I'll see you Tuesday night then."

"Seven sharp." He answered and headed to his truck. The drive back to the Ensconce, the diner/club he owned, was short. Parking around the back, he sat for a minute and took a breath. He'd worked hard the last ten years making this place what it was now. At sixteen years old, he was sort of a hothead. He was the best shooting guard statewide in basketball. The popularity and demand for him got him in a little bit of trouble. After the state championship game, a fight ended with several of his team members, including him, sentenced to one hundred hours of volunteer work or community service. While most other boys choose community service, his dad found him a job, working for Roger Mack at Mack's Diner. As a busboy. That was his job for two months. He wanted to argue with his dad. As a high school basketball star, cleaning tables and dishes at his mother's request was one thing but, in an environment where people could see him and tease him, that was embarrassing. His father didn't budge, and he had too much respect for his father to ever go against the instruction.

Claiming it would teach him some humility and knock some of that pride out of him. He didn't understand it at first, and the first two weeks were hell. He'd tried to pick hours when the least amount of high school kids would be in and out of the diner, but the weekend proved to be useless, and eventually, everyone knew he was working at Mack's as a busboy.

His saving grace came one afternoon while cleaning tables. Alexia Stevens. She walked into the diner with Shayna and Kaycee, and they took a booth near a table he was cleaning. Calling him over to take a break, Kaycee and Shayna discussed Shayna's most recent encounter with his brother Jerome. The second oldest. It wasn't a secret that he and Shayna had a falling out in high school and were deemed arch enemies since. It still shocked him they were married now. Kaycee, married to his brother James, the closest to him, despite the six-year gap, was happy to finally be able to have a break away from his one-year niece. Alexia was visiting, planning to attend the annual masquerade ball. She'd moved out to California after her mom died, but the three of them remained best friends. It had been his opening up to

Alexia about the diner being embarrassing and practically boring that sparked Alexia to suggest that he makes the best of it and consider talking to Mr. Mack about some changes and upgrades. The conversation led from one idea to the next, and the simple diner became the number one teenage spot in the city. His two months of bussing tables turned into two years, and then one year of business management. He kept playing basketball, but the appeal of making pro lost its touch. Especially after he'd come up with the idea to turn the diner's basement into an underground club. Officially changing the name to Ensconce. It had all started with Alexia. He'd put her on a pedestal and kept her there for years, earning her the nickname of 'Jacen's Lexi'. Most thought his crush and idealization of her was a joke, but he'd loved her or at least what she had represented to him. Dreams, hope, ambition. Coming down from that high had been hard when he found out she was dating his oldest brother, Justin. When she'd moved back to Boston, he'd been so focused and making sure the club was up and running that he'd missed it. His pride had almost cost him his friendship with his brother. It took months after finally seeing how truly in love they both were together to finally accept he honestly didn't love Alexia, at least not for who she was. But of the dream girl, he imagined her to be. He dated a lot of women after that. Always upfront, never one to hide his true intention or his motives. His reputation almost exceeded his brother Jerome's pre-Shayna days.

He ran his hand down his face bringing his thoughts back to the present. He needed to focus on getting a new investor. But with the events coming up with the charity calendar, another issue he didn't want to concentrate on plague the front of his mind. Chelsea. She invaded his thoughts more than he wanted. It seemed like a simple arrangement. He just needed a date for all the events for the calendar. No drama, no expectation, and then everyone goes their separate ways with a clean slate. Chelsea's hesitation made him think about his past with other women. Most of the women in Boston or in the tri-city radius could care less about his history or any woman he dated before them. He honestly never considered a woman having the opposite reaction. The more he thought about it, the more it made sense for a girl like Chelsea not to jump at the opportunity. That made him nervous. If she decided to turn his offer down, he wouldn't have a date for the calendar events, including the charity ball. Shayna's head would fly off her shoulders if he showed up without a date. He was sure of it. But if he were honest, if he couldn't have Chelsea, Jacen didn't want anyone else, and that thought alone let him know if she agreed, the arrangement wouldn't be as simple as he thought.

Chapter Four

"Chelsea, it's so good to see you." Shayna exclaimed as she engulfed Chelsea in a hug. Chelsea smiled, accepting the loving embrace of her former boss.

"It's good to see you also Shayna. How are Jerome and Miracle doing?"

"Well, Miracle is growing like a weed. I still can't believe she'll be twelve next year."

"She is growing up to be quite the little lady, I see."

"Yes, she is. So, what brings you to the shoot today? I didn't see your name on the volunteer list."

"I'm actually here as Jacen's date." she admitted nervously. Remembering her phone to Jacen. He was pleasantly surprised by her decision. They discussed going on a few dates outside the calendar events, and Chelsea also mentioned the flight detail and arrangements made by her family once they arrived for the wedding. Jacen teased her about being the best boyfriend and asked her what kind of gifts she liked. Chelsea declined to receive any gifts, but absentmindedly mention that she'd never received flowers from a man before.

"Really?" Shayna responded in an expression Chelsea could not make out.

"That's not a problem, is it?" she asked, curious about Shayna's opinion. Shayna blinked as if realizing she hadn't answered her.

"Of course not. Asia." Shayna turned and called out, and a young girl wearing a sewing apron appeared. "This is Chelsea Stone. She will be our bachelor's date for this years' calendar events."

"It's nice to meet Ms. Stone. Asia said, extending her hand.

"You can call me Chelsea. It's wonderful to meet you as well, Asia." Chelsea said, accepting the handshake.

"Please make sure to measure Chelsea for all the costumes we've planned for this year. Shayna instructed.

"Yes, Mrs. Turner. Chelsea, if you would please follow me." Asia suggested.

"I will see you in a little while Chelsea." Shayna stated as she walked down an opposite hall in the community center. Chelsea watched her retreat and wondered if Shayna had an issue with her as Jacen's date.

"Chelsea?" Asia reminded her she hadn't moved from her spot.

"I'm sorry, Asia, lead the way." the young lady smiled as she led Chelsea to the art and crafts room. It was full of tables with props, costumes, skims for changing, and scene backdrops.

"Wow. Shayna's outdoing herself this year." Chelsea said.

"Most of these items are donated from the drama program at Boston U." Asia replied.

"They have an excellent program, from what I remember."

"Did you attend Boston U?" Asia asked while taking Chelsea's measurements.

"I did. That's how I met Shayna. I did an internship at Show Stoppin' Magazine."

"That is so cool. I used to love that magazine." Asia admitted. The two of them continued to conversate as Asia continued to measure her. Asia also informed Chelsea of the photoshoot schedule and some of the intended costumes. There were four photoshoots scheduled and a bonus one just in case of weather issues affecting two of them planned outdoors. Two charity events were planned, the annual cookie drive at the Children's Shelter and the Annual Charity Ball held at the governor's mansion.

"I think we have all of your measurements." Asia stated.

"Am I done?" Chelsea asked.

"With me, yes. I am to direct you go to the cafeteria where I think a posing coach will assist you."

"A posing coach?" Chelsea questioned.

"Yes, I can never remember her name. Do you know where the cafeteria is?"

"I do." Chelsea said. She thanked Asia and headed out of the room. The cafeteria was on the other side of the community center, and just as she was passing the entrance, Jacen walked in. He was shaking the lapel of his coat and stomping his feet on the rug to get the snow off.

"I guess it started snowing." she said. He looked up, meeting her eyes.

"It did." he confirmed as he walked over to her. "How are you, Chelsea?"

"I'm good. A young girl named Asia just took my measurements. She's down this hall if you need to see her." she said, pointing in the direction she'd just come from.

"I sent Shayna my measurements weeks ago."

"You already knew your measurements?" she asked, surprised.

"I gave her the same ones I received when I was measured for my tux for Trent's wedding." he answered.

"Oh." she said, nodding.

"Where are you heading?" He asked.

"The cafeteria. I am supposed to work with a posing coach."

"That's always fun." he said dryly. "I have to see Shayna before I head that way."

"I think Asia mentioned her being in one of the staff offices."

"Then I guess I'll see you later." He said.

"Alright." she answered and turned to head toward the cafeteria.

~~~~~~~~~~~~~~~~~~~~~~~~

Jacen watched Chelsea walk down the hall toward the cafeteria for a moment before he walked straight ahead to find Shayna. He smiled realizing he made Chelsea nervous. Very few women were nervous around him. Most were overconfident, comfortable in their interaction with him as if they had the right to be at his side. Chelsea did not act entitled when around him. She was pleasant, shy at times, and everyone enjoyed her presence, both his staff and his family. Her closeness with his family was the reason he was meeting with Shayna. He'd texted her he was running late. He had spent a little longer than expected working on applying for the permit on the new location. The moment Shayna responded they needed to talk, he knew Chelsea had arrived at the community center. He didn't regret his choice in selecting her. She was supposed to be a safe choice, and she still was, or at least he thought she was. His attraction to her should send up smoke signals and red flags, but it had accomplished the opposite. He was honestly looking forward to dating Chelsea.

"Jacen ramped his knuckle on the office door announcing his presence as Shayna lifted her head from her laptop.

"You've finally made it." she stated. He chuckled.

"It started snowing." he said, taking off his jacket and hanging it on the back of a chair as he took a seat.

"I'm sure this could go without saying, but I'm going to say it anyway." she began. Jacen nodded but didn't speak. He was very aware of what she was going to say.

"Do not hurt Chelsea, Jacen." she warned.

"I don't intend to."

"Intending to and doing are very different things."

"I know that Shayna, but how do you know I won't be the one that ends up hurt?"' he asked jokingly. She didn't smile.

"This isn't a joke, Jacen." she said more sternly. Apart from him wanted to tell her to mind her own business. What happened between him, and Chelsea was between them, but he knew better. Shayna was acting as a surrogate protective sister, which he understood. Another reason was he didn't want to have to deal with Jerome. Where Justin and James might be forgiving when it came to crossing their wives, Jerome Turner was not. And the last thing he needed was his brother at his doorstep. Jacen had to tread lightly as he answer Shayna.

"What are you worried about, Shayna? I've known Chelsea for years. I'm not playing any games with her. I like her." he said honestly, discovering how much that was true with each passing day. Shayna's brow lifted slightly before she spoke.

"I'll let this go, for now." she announced. She pulled a folder out and handed it to him. The schedule for the photoshoots, location, and themes were on it. There were only two mandatory events he would have with Chelsea. The others he could do solo. He also needed to complete and approve her interview questions and select his charity of choice for the calendar proceeds to go to. They spoke for a while on a few other things before he left her office and went looking for Chelsea. He found her interestingly concentrating on balancing on a very thin stool. The choreographer was explaining due to their height difference in certain shots, she would need to be elevated. He smiled as he watched. She seemed very uncomfortable, concerned with falling, but determined and listening attentively to the instructions given.

"Jacen, why didn't you come on over here for a second." the choreographer said, noticing his entrance into the old cafeteria that was set up with various backdrops, lighting fixtures, and multiple style cameras.

"I'm all yours. Where do you want me?" he said.

"Please stand here." she instructed. Her name was Marta. She spoke in a tone that belied her age. The younger woman was very professional. Dressing in a light gray pants suit, her hair pulled up in a neat bun and small pearl earrings in her ears. It was a complete contrast to Chelsea's soft pink cashmere sweater and nice-fitting jeans. Her sandy brown hair pulled into a side ponytail and rested just below her collar bone. Jacen struggled to pay attention as his gaze continued to focus on Chelsea and not Marta. She'd cleared her throat a few times to get his attention. He apologized and worked hard to pay attention for the rest of their session. An hour later, he and Chelsea were free from the pre-photo shoot session.

"Where are you headed?" Jacen asked as he helped Chelsea put on her coat.

"To the diner." she answered. He lifted a brow.

"I seriously needed to put you on staff."

"It's fine. I don't mind helping. What about you? Are you going to take the night off? The club isn't opening." he smiled at her question. The club wasn't open tonight. It was one of the things he loved about Wednesdays. Usually, he could have a whole night off.

"Actually, I'm supposed to be doing a few talent interviews."

"Oh?" she asked.

"I'm thinking about bringing amateur night back." Amateur night had been something Mr. Mack had started a few years before handing the diner over to Jacen. It was a small platform and a microphone setup. He recalled rearranging the chairs in the diner after hours on Thursdays nights for the show.

"Really?" she said, her eyes lightening up with excitement.

"Yes, I've gotten a lot of inquiries and some major local talent. I'm thinking of even adding some local comedians." Jacen said. The current theatre that housed most of the comedy events was remodeling the next few months. The major events were rescheduled to locations upstate.

"Jacen, that sounds exciting. Can I help?"

"Chelsea, you help me enough as it is. I'm going to have an extremely large tab." He joked as they walked in the afternoon brisk to their vehicles.

"Well, I don't mind, just let me know." she said, opening her car door.

"If you really want to, just come down after the dinner rush." he responded, holding her door as she sat in her car.

"Okay."

"I'll follow you to the diner."

"Alright." she said as he closed her door and walked over to his own vehicle.

~~~~~~~~~~~~~~~~~~~~~~~~

"I haven't laughed so hard in a long time. Jacen has some serious talent lined up." Chelsea announced as she brought the big bowl of popcorn from her kitchen and plopped down on the couch beside Ashiree.

"I think it's great that Jacen is bringing Amateur night back." Ashiree agreed.

"Yes, I think it will be nice for everyone."

"So, the wedding is this weekend?"

"Yes." Chelsea answered with a sigh. She wasn't too confident about attending her sister's wedding. However, she was slightly excited about seeing her dad.

"Are you nervous?" Ashiree asked with genuine concern.

"A little. I haven't seen Sonica in years, Ronica and I barely speak, and you know my situation with Monica." Ashiree nodded her head.

"Makes me grateful at times I didn't have a family."

"Ashiree!" Chelsea said, appalled, and threw popcorn at her.

"What? It's true." she said, laughing while dodging popcorn kernels.

"That is not something to joke about." Chelsea protested.

"Hey, sometimes you have to laugh at life's shortcomings." Ashiree responded. Chelsea shook her head at her.

"Just pick a movie for us to watch and no Netflix series either." Ashiree rolled her eyes at her, but Chelsea ignored it. She liked movies and wasn't a binger like her best friend. Ashiree could binge anything, especially right after a semester ended. It was how she winded down. Chelsea could admit she liked the show Reign on Netflix until the abrupt ending of season five. She was done binging after that, such a disappointment. Ashiree chose an action-adventure film and a suspense thriller. She wasn't big on romance or drama films. Chelsea didn't mind since she'd edited two romance novels that week, getting her fix of happily ever after. Halfway through the suspense thriller, Chelsea noticed her friend curled up on the other side of the couch, asleep. She smiled and finished watching the movie.

Once it was over, she grabbed a blanket and covered her friend. Remembering the first time they had their first sleepover. It was by pure accident after a chocolate overdose. She chuckled quietly, recalling how worried Ashiree's foster mom had been and how angry her aunt had been over them eating up her brownie batter. Chelsea picked up the near-empty popcorn bowl and took it to the kitchen. Cutting out the lights and the TV, she headed to her bedroom on the second floor. Sliding under her covers, she thought about the other day, the upcoming photoshoot, scoping out the talent with Jacen for Amateur night; she loved it. Watching Jacen laugh had been the highlight of it all. His laugh was rich and deep. She had it bad. How she ever planned to survive, she had no idea. Ashiree told her to go for the gold and enjoy every moment she could. She even suggested packing some nice lingerie for the wedding weekend. Chelsea had no plans on seducing Jacen. She wanted him to see her like he saw other women, well maybe not exactly like other women, but she wanted him to notice her. She was playing a dangerous game and one that could leave her heart in shambles. But wasn't that what the heroines in romance novels did? Put their hearts on the lines for a men they wanted? She scoffed at the thought. She didn't live in a happily ever after novel. Most of the heroines she read about the men desired them from the beginning. She'd known Jacen Turner for nearly eight years, and he never noticed her. Chelsea was way too hopeful to think that would change, but she could enjoy the time she had and pray when it was over; her heart was still intact, and she could still be his friend.

Chapter Five

"So, when was the last time you were home?" Jacen asked as they arrived at the airport.

"A few years, not since my oldest sister got married."

"I didn't even know you had sisters. How come you never talk about them?" Jacen asked. Chelsea sighed. She didn't talk about the other side of her family, the side that hated her. Well, maybe hate was a strong word to describe Sonica and Ronica's feelings towards her, but Monica definitely hated her. There was never an easy way to talk about the relationship with her sister or lack thereof. The safest way had been to avoid it altogether. It allowed for discussion of past situations she never wanted to remember from being talked about.

"We're not that close." she said, placing her luggage on the conveyor belt.

"I'm sure there's a story behind that."

"There always is." She answered dryly, and one she would not be telling. Making through security, then both stopped at a small coffee shop. After ordering cups of coffee and a few pastries, they noticed a small table in the back. Chelsea knew Jacen was trying not to laugh as she attempted to hop up on the stool. After she finally was able to get situated in her seat, she smiled back at him, trying not to laugh also.

"Hey, short people problems." She explained.

"Maybe next time, I'll just pick you up." She blushed, averting her eyes from him and looking at her coffee cup as she brought it to her lips.

"We're going to have to work on that."

"What?"

"You, blushing every time, I flirt with you."

"Or you could not flirt with me."

"What kind of boyfriend would I be without flirting with you." She nodded in agreement but didn't have a comeback. Her boyfriend. When he first agreed, she could admit she was shocked, then confused, then nervous. A jumble of emotions flooded her insides after their talk in his office. Ashiree insisted she make their relationship as real as possible and ordered several different types of lingerie online for her to pack. Chelsea didn't pack any of them. This weekend was not the time to enter into an intimate relationship with Jacen. But the thought wasn't unpleasant. Who was she kidding? The idea was very pleasant and one she wished she could fully act on, but knew she didn't have the courage to do so.

"Hey, penny for your thoughts?" Jacen asked, interrupting her internal rambling.

"Sorry, just thinking about something?"

"Are you nervous about this weekend?" he asked.

"A little."

"Is there anything I should be worried about?"

"No, no, I'm sure you'll be fine."

"Okay, so which sister is getting married again?"

"Sonica. She's traveled the world doing missionary work for different organizations for women's rights and equality."

"Sonica, that's a different name, and is she the youngest? Well before you?"

"No, that's Monica. We're only a year apart. Sonica is older than me by three years, and Ronica is a year older than her."

"Sonica, Ronica and Monica. Okay, then, somebody likes rhymes."

"More of someone wanting their children basically named after them."

"I can't think of another name that rhymes with those." Jacen responded, his eyes deepening in thought.

"Try Onica."

"Onica? Like the model and actress Onica Devereaux?"

"The one and only." Chelsea said, not wanting to get into her stepmother and her overcompensating lifestyle.

"Wow, so you all must share the same dad?" Chelsea nodded, watching the play of emotions on Jacen's face as the pieces of this very twisted puzzle called her life, was about to come together. Three, two, one...

"Fredrick Stone is your dad?" Bingo! He nailed it in one guess. Hardly anyone made the connection between her and her former actor/ movie executive producer father. Stone wasn't an uncommon name, and since her mother was black and Chelsea lived in Boston, most people didn't consider they were related. Jacen rested back on his stool as the magnitude of her parentage sunk in.

"Wow. Chelsea. I feel like I don't even know you now."

"It's not something I like to talk about." She wasn't one to drop names or bring up celebrities in conversations. Besides, that part of her life was practically non-existent.

"Does anyone know? Ashiree? Shayna even?"

"Ashiree knows. If Shayna knew, she never said anything. I know a background check was conducted when I started working for Show Stoppin', so it's possible, but we've never discussed it." She wasn't necessarily hiding who her father was; she just chose not to mention it. The silence hung between them as she watched Jacen process the bomb of information he discovered about her. She wondered if he somehow felt betrayed or maybe uncomfortable around her now. Chelsea was about to ask him how he felt, as he finished the last of his danish and coffee, but the announcement of their flight prompted them to discard the last of their food items and head to the gate.

~~~~~~~~~~~~~~~~~~~~~~~~~

Frederick Stone's daughter. She was Fredrick Stone's daughter? She acted like that was just some regular guy around the corner. The man and his family were Hollywood royalty, keeping Hollywood alive for the last fifty years. What else didn't he know about her? Why was she living in Boston? In a three-story brownstone, no less. Not that he was condemning her choice of where to live. He knew the brownstone belonged to her aunt, and it was left to her when she passed, but there was no way she couldn't afford to live in a more high-end class of the city. Unless somehow Fredrick Stone cast aside his youngest daughter, that the world knew nothing about. Taking his seat in first class now made sense. He hadn't considered it before when they arrived. Chelsea simply said her family made the arrangements, and he assumed they were generous and happy she was attending the wedding. He sent the last text he needed to his manager and club security before turning it off on the plane. The weekends were always busiest for him. The diner in the morning and the club at night. He hadn't realized he never took a weekend off or at least away. So much went into ensuring everything went smoothly while he was in Florida. Pensacola, to be exact. He'd never been there. Heard it was beautiful and like no other city and practically surrounded by water, almost feeling like an island. He planned to enjoy the climate change, leaving the brisk October weather in Boston to the post-hurricane warmth of Pensacola. Arriving at Pensacola International Airport, he was thankful for the first-class seating. At 6'4', his height sometimes caused discomfort when seated in a plane. As he and Chelsea exited the plane and headed to baggage claim, he felt they needed to talk. It took a while for him to process what she'd told him. He'd known Chelsea for almost eight years or thought he knew her. It made him question whether or not they had really been friends. Or more so had he been a friend to her. The plane ride gave him time to think about his actions or interest in her before the agreement they made. When Chelsea started working for Shayna, he never considered more to her than what he saw on the surface. Shayna always included Chelsea in things with him and his family, outside of them working together. She got along with everyone and was even present for the births of some of his nieces and nephews. He knew his mother had formed a friendship with her aunt before she died, bringing Chelsea further into their family fold. He watched her as they waited for their luggage to appear on the carousel. She was texting someone on her phone. Having an opportunity to just admire her, he took in her light caramel complexion, her sandy brown hair that she pulled into a ponytail. Even standing in her wedge heels, she barely reached his shoulder. He took a brief moment to stop staring at her in time to see their luggage circling them. Quickly grabbing both suitcases. Chelsea informed them a car would be waiting for them outside. A car? She said it like it was the most natural thing in the world. Sure this was her family, but he noticed slight changes in Chelsea's posture and demeanor. Typically she was so relaxed and easygoing. Now she looked stoic and conservative. A look on her he'd never seen before. Following her outside, he was immediately hit with muggy humidity from the heat that engulfed them.

"It's like stepping into a sauna." He said and quickly grabbed his shades.

"Yes, just take some slow breaths, and you'll be alright." She said, smiling for the first time since they left Boston.

"Ms. Chelsea?" They both turned to find a man in a white suit, aviator shades, and standing next to a limo.

"Jasper? On my goodness, it's so good to see you." Chelsea practically ran the few steps they were away from Jasper. Jacen's first twinge of jealousy began to spike, which he quickly toned down. The man was practically twice his age, but he honestly hadn't liked the sight of Chelsea in another mans' arms. Where had that come from? He wasn't the jealous type. He never staked claim to a woman. He chucked it up as him taking on the role of being her boyfriend seriously. Walking over to them with the luggage. Jasper released Chelsea from his grasp.

"Jasper this Jacen Turner, Jacen this is Jasper, he's worked for my father for years."

"Too many years. Wonderful to meet you son." He said, extending his hand in greeting.

"You are also." Jacen replied. Taking his hand in a firm handshake.

"Well, let me take those bags. You two kids hop on in the back." Jacen lifted an eyebrow at being called a kid. Chelsea seemed completely unbothered by it and entered the limo as Jasper took their luggage to the trunk. Jacen took a seat in the back while Chelsea sat on the side seat.

"A limo?" He asked, gaining her attention.

"I know. It's a little different." Her cheery disposition puzzled him.

"You seem happier all of a sudden." He said.

"I know. I honestly have been dreading this weekend. But seeing Jasper just lifted my spirits. He was always nice to me, and my aunt too." Her tone dropped a little in the last part.

"I feel like it's a completely different side of you that I know nothing about."

"Most people don't. I prefer not to talk about my past."

"I feel as your boyfriend I should know all your secrets." He said with a smirk.

"Pulling the boyfriend card on me already?"

"Is it working?"

"No." she said, shaking her head, but smiled teasingly at him.

"You two are all situated back there." Jasper asked, sitting in the driver's seat of the limo.

"We're good to go, Jasper." Chelsea voiced.

"Do you want the privacy screen up? I ain't one for stopping no hanky panky from you youngsters."

"Jasper!" Chelsea exclaimed, appalled with complete shock on her face. Jacen threw his head back in laughter. He wasn't sure if he would like Jasper until that very moment.

Chapter Six

The ride to her father's mansion seemed short, with Jacen and Jasper talking the entire ride. She was happy to see Jacen more at ease after finding out who her father was. It wasn't something she talked about with anyone besides Ashiree. She'd mentioned it once while in college, and several people, guys, and girls asked about the movie industry and how they could get an interview with her dad or the inside scoop to be an extra in the next movie he produced. Thank goodness social media wasn't popular then. She'd never be able to live her life in peace. The lifestyle of the rich and famous was not all it was jazzed up to be. She knew the ugly side, the hurtful side. The side that chose to keep a specific image to the public at the expense of doing what was right. Chelsea leaned forward as Jasper pulled into the gated community and looked through the front window as the mansion came into view. It always reminded her of a castle as a little girl. She always dreamed of her prince charming coming to save her from it. Looks could be deceiving. The prettiest castles usually held the worst dungeons.

"Welcome home, Ms. Chelsea." Jasper said as he parked the limo in front of the two-story beige mansion. Chelsea smiled but didn't respond. She glanced over at Jacen, who had his neck cocked to the side as he looked through the tinted glass. Jasper came around to open the door, and after Jacen stepped out, he turned, offering his hand to assist her.

"Thank you." Chelsea looked up at him as she took his hand. She was surprised by his offer of assistance, but then she thought better of it. Jacen was always a perfect gentleman.

"What do you think?" She asked him as they stood staring up at the house.

"It's nice. Reminds me a little of the Taylor estate, with all the windows." She nodded in agreement. She'd been invited to the childhood home of his best friend Trent only once. Now that she thought about it, Trent's mother, Constance, and Onica would get along well.

"Oh my goodness! Chelsea! You actually came." Chelsea laughed as she saw her childhood friend approach.

"Lorelai. It's good to see you." She said as Lorelai quickly grabbed her in for a hug.

"It's been way too long. How are you? And who is this tall drink of water?" Lorelai winked at Jacen, and Chelsea laughed. Lorelai hadn't changed a bit. She flirted even when they were kids, and the same held true now.

"Lorelai, this is Jacen. Jacen, this is my oldest friend Lorelai."

"It's nice to meet you." Jacen said, extending his hand to Lorelai but placing his other around Chelsea's waist.

"The pleasure is definitely all mine. I see Chelsea already has her claim on you, but you wouldn't happen to have any brothers, would you?"

"Three brothers actually, and they're all married." Jacen answered.

"Well, just break a girls' heart, why don't you?" Lorelai brought her hand to her chest in a dramatic gesture as if she were just stabbed in the heart.

"Don't mind her or her theatrics." Chelsea said to Jacen, laughing at Lorelai.

"Oh sweetie, the theatrics have yet to begin." Chelsea groaned, knowing full well what or who Lorelai was referring to.

"Monica."

"Yes, honey. The wicked witch of the south has her broomstick prepped and ready to wreak havoc on all of Pensacola." Lorelai answered.

"Now, don't you start spreading rumors, Lorelai. We have guests." Jasper said from behind them, nodding his head over to Jacen.

"No one should be subject to entering the witch's den without warning." Lorelai replied. Jasper and Chelsea both shook their heads at Lorelai, but Chelsea knew she wasn't too far off the mark. Her youngest sister was a pill.

"I'll just take these to your room Ms. Chelsea, and you behave yourself. We don't need you scaring off the guest." Jasper said, eyeing Lorelai, who completely ignored his warning.

"Awe, you don't look like you scare easily, do you, honey?" She said, addressing Jacen.

"No, not easily." Jacen replied.

"See, nothing to worry about, Jasper." She called out to him as he made his way around the side of the house through the servants' quarters.

"Well, come along, you two, everyone's waiting for you by the pool." Lorelai began ascending the stairs up to the front door. Jacen leaned down to whisper in Chelsea's ears as they followed Lorelai.

"Who is the wicked witch of the south?"

"My sister, Monica."

"Should I be worried?"

"No. She only hates me." Chelsea answered. She knew Jacen wanted to ask more questions, and she figured she would need to explain some things to him at some point. Hopefully not all at once. There were some secrets she wanted to keep buried, some things she never wanted to talk about, some things Chelsea wished she could forget.

~~~~~~~~~~~~~~~~~~~~~~

She only hates me. Those words didn't sit well with Jacen. Chelsea said them as if they were the natural way for her sister to feel about her. He couldn't imagine it. His older brothers teased him while he was younger. It was no secret that he had been a surprise to his parents, thinking they were done having kids, rendering him the nickname the "oops baby". But it was a joke. None of his brothers ever made him feel as though they didn't truly like him. They supported him, loved him, especially at times when he honestly didn't deserve it. He had the

~ 73 ~

best relationship with his oldest brother Justin now, despite his immaturity, stubbornness, and pride, which almost kept Justin and Alexia apart. Knowing how happy they are now, seeing the true love that flowed between them and welcoming his nephew into the world, he knew his actions had been childish, selfish, and could have caused a major rift in his family. Luckily, he'd smarten up in time, realize how truly in love they were, and accepted he wasn't the man for Alexia. Once he got over his pride being bruised and began to explain to his family how he wanted to create a nightclub out of the large basement below the diner, Justin had been the first one to step up and help. He found a new level of respect for him. Holding nothing back, his oldest brother walked him through every step of what would be needed for the architectural design and stability measures required to convert it. At that moment, Jacen knew the man he respected and looked up to most after his father was Justin.

Walking through the mansion while holding Chelsea's hand, Lorelai prompted as somewhat of a tour guide, explaining all the pictures on the walls of various celebrities and politicians. She also explained how each room displayed a theme depending on Onica's taste when she decided to decorate it. Jacen looked around at the grandeur in complete awe. The painting sculptures the ceiling-high vases with African markings on them. The excessive decor and design put the Taylor Manor to shame. He didn't think anyone could outdo Constance Taylor's style or extreme taste. But he was wrong. Onica Devereaux had Constance beat hand over fist. Now walking down a hallway covered in glass windows and looking out into the gulf, Jacen stopped to enjoy the view.

"Wow. This view alone would be worth it." He said out loud, talking to no one in particular. His home back in Boston gave him a decent view of the harbor, and he loved going out on his deck just to stare out and listen to the sounds of the city as the boats passed along the waters. But the view he was witnessing now put a major dim on the one he had.

"I'm sure you'll get an up-close view when Mr. Stone takes the men out on his new boat tomorrow." Lorelai said, taking in the site with him and Chelsea.

"Daddy got a new boat?" Jacen heard Chelsea ask Lorelai.

"Yup, his new pride and joy." Lorelai answered.

"What happened to Sadie?" Chelsea asked.

"He sold it to Casey." He saw Lorelai roll her eyes at the mention of Casey, but what caught his attention was the slight stiffening he felt in Chelsea's grip. *Who was Casey?* He thought.

"Come on, they're all waiting." Jacen saw Chelsea hesitate and then held her head up and proceeded to follow Lorelai again. She never let go of his hand. He knew they were to appear as a happy couple, but he was certain she kept hold of it for the support he was beginning to think she needed. Continuing walking hand and hand, they came to a door at the end of the hallway, and Lorelai happily opened it for them, allowing Chelsea and himself to walk through.

"Chelsea! You made it." Jacen watched as a tall blonde-haired woman walked over to them, followed by two other women and two men.

"I wasn't going to miss your wedding Sonica." Chelsea said as she accepted the hug from the bride-to-be. Sonica beamed in delight, looking down at Chelsea.

"I'm so happy you're here." Her voice croaked, and Jacen could see she was on the brink of tears.

"Good Lord Sonica, don't you start crying. My pregnancy hormones can't take it, and then I'll be crying too." Sonica wiped a tear away as she was slightly pushed out of the way for another sister to hug Chelsea. He could see her slight baby bump under the swimsuit cover-up she had on as she engulfed Chelsea in a hug as well.

"It really is good to see you." Ronica said.

"You too, Ronica. I see you have a little extra weight there." Jacen heard Chelsea say. Ronica rolled her eyes and nodded her head toward one of the men behind them.

"Garrett there, just couldn't wait to get me pregnant."

"And I'm unashamed of it." Garrett said, looking at his wife, then extended his hand to Jacen.

"I'm Garrett Winslow." Jacen accepted it with a firm shake.

"Jacen Turner."

"Oh, I'm sorry. Everyone, this is Jacen Turner, Jacen these are my sisters Sonica, Ronica, and Monica." He greeted both older sisters as they happily greeted each other. All the women favored one another in both height, hair, and body type. However, Jacen immediately noticed one of them looked closer to Chelsea's twin, despite the blonde hair. It seemed the sister Chelsea claimed to hate her was the one that resembled her the most. The other two held a striking resemblance to their mother, Onica. Monica's greeting was cold, and she did not extend her hand to him as she sipped from the champagne glass in her hand.

"And this is my soon-to-be husband, Nigel." Sonica proudly exclaimed. Jacen and Nigel exchanged greetings and handshakes.

"Well, let's all go have a seat, and you can fill us in on your life in Boston. From the looks of things, I'd say it's going pretty well." Sonica said before leading them over to the section of chairs and loungers in the sitting room. Another wall of windows was lined on one side, and Jacen could see an indoor pool.

"Turner, huh?" Garrett said with one eyebrow arched. "From Boston?"

"Yes." Jacen answered, accepting a glass of champagne for both himself and Chelsea while that sat. He wasn't big on drinking, but he wasn't going to be rude. Chelsea took a big gulp as soon as she accepted the glass from him, and with the death stares both of them were receiving from Monica, he began to understand why.

"You wouldn't happen to be related to James Turner, the attorney, would you?" Garret asked.

"Yes. He's, my brother." Jacen answered.

"Well, I'll be. That brother of yours is a beast in the courtroom." Garret exclaimed. Jacen chuckled. Yes, James was pretty amazing.

"Who is this?" Nigel asked. As the others did, Jacen listened to Garrett's account of James' cases and career success. A few years ago, James took on a case in Hollywood against a very sought out actor that was blackmailing one of his one-night stands into having an abortion. No Hollywood attorney would touch the case. James was still considered a rookie back then, but he'd won that case, making a name for himself and still ranked as one of the top ten most desired lawyers in the country.

"That's pretty impressive." Nigel commented, placing his around Sonica in the seat next to him.

"So, what line of business are you in, Jacen?" Ronica asked. She chose one of the loungers, which allowed her to lay back and place her feet on Garrett's lap.

"I own a diner and nightclub." He heard a disapproving sound from Monica as she finished her glass, signaling the maid to bring her another drink. Chelsea accepted another glass of champagne as well. She hadn't spoken since they'd sat down and the tension in the air hung deep, even with Garrett and Ronica attempting to make small talk.

"How did you get into that?" Jacen quickly recapped how he came to own the diner and eventually turned the basement storage into a nightclub, leaving out the part about him starting there initially for community service.

"That's pretty impressive." Garrett responded. The silence grew between them for just a second before Sonica broke the ice.

"So, how long have you and Chelsea been dating?" Jacen looked at Chelsea as she glanced over at him, both smiling slightly. He knew that this question would come up, but neither of them went over exactly how to respond to it. Luckily, the door to the sitting-room opened, and they were saved, or so he thought. None other than Hollywood royalty Fredrick Stone walked through the door.

Chapter Seven

Chelsea stood the minute she saw her father and began walking over to greet him.

"I thought I heard bells ringing." Chelsea laughed as she engulfed herself in her father's arms. Chel Bells was her nickname, and she indulged in all his corny jokes referencing bells whenever she was around him.

"Hi, daddy." She said, taking in the cool water scent only familiar to him. He always smelled the same unless he smoked a cigar. Despite all the things that went on in their past, she still loved her father. She wouldn't consider herself a daddy's girl, but she was close enough.

"It looks like Boston is treating you well." Fredrick said while releasing her.

"It is." She felt Jacen's presence before she turned to see him coming to stand next to her.

"And who is this strapping young man?" His father asked in a light tone.

"Jacen Turner sir." Chelsea watched as her father shook Jacen's extended hand.

"A firm handshake and manners, I like this one." Her father looked at her and then back at Jacen. She was keenly aware of Jacen's height in comparison to her father. He stood proud at 5'11' and was in pretty good shape in his mid-sixties, but Jacen standing in all his 6' 4' glory, broad, sturdy shoulders, solid chest, and ripped arms, put all the other men in the room to shame. Chelsea blinked; how much champagne did she drink? Did she just ogle Jacen in front of her father? Jacen and her father were discussing something when the door opened again, and Onica walked into the sitting room with Casey. Chelsea instantly froze and tried to calm her nerves. She obviously hadn't done a good job because she felt Jacen place his arm slowly around her waist. She looked up at him and soon regretted it. The look of concern on his face let her know she hadn't done a great job of masking her reaction to seeing Casey. He looked over at Casey then back at her, and she knew from the shift in his jawline that he'd picked up on her nerves and knew something was wrong.

"Well, Chelsea. It is good to see you. I didn't think you'd make it." Onica's greeting was as fake as the nose and lips she had done on her face. However, focusing on Onica made it a lot easier than concentrating on Casey.

"And who is this?" Onica said coyly. The tone in her voice was anything but fake. Where Chelsea could ignore Lorelai's harmless flirting with Jacen, Onica's reputation of being an avid cougar didn't sit well with her. She didn't believe that Jacen would be interested in Onica for one second, she was practically old enough to be his mother, but she couldn't stop the twinge of jealousy that sparked in her. Jacen's grip on her waist tightened as he also seemed to notice the direct intent in Onica's voice.

"I'm Jacen Turner, Chelsea's boyfriend." He said proudly and firmly.

"Well, she seems to have good taste." Onica said with a slow wink. Chelsea's anger didn't get a chance to rise up in her as Casey decided to speak right after Onica.

"Boyfriend, huh? I'm Casey Worthington. Chelsea's brother-in-law." Chelsea almost cringed the way he said her name. Any jealousy or anger due to Onica's blatant flirting with Jacen subsided in just hearing Casey speak. She hated this feeling, why she hardly ever visited her father, and continued to keep Sonia and Ronica at arm's length.

"Jacen Turner." She heard Jacen say again in greeting. His voice was sterner than when he'd spoken to Onica. She knew he felt the tension in her body due to Casey's presence. He allowed her to lean into him for the comfort she needed. She was sure he would ask questions later. But right now, she just wanted to get through introductions. Eventually, they all retook their seats while Monica continued giving her death stares, completely ignoring the opposite looks Casey was giving her. It was like no one, but she and Jacen noticed. It was the main reason she didn't want to come here alone and kept her away for years at a time.

"So, Jacen Turner. Tell us about yourself." Casey said in a mocking tone. Before he could say anything, Garrett spoke. Talking about Jacen and adding in all the success of his older brother James.

"Are you related to Justin Turner also?" Casey asked, trying not to jump on Jacen's bandwagon as Garrett had.

"The architect?" Her father asked, shockingly.

"Yes, sir." Jacen's tone was light when speaking to her father, but his face was clear on his mistrust for Casey.

"Just how many brothers do you have?" Monica asked, seeming to finally find her voice with her husband's cynical attitude toward Jacen.

"I have three." Jacen answered as calmly as he could. Chelsea could feel the rigidness in his body as Monia, Casey, and Onica's presence began to settle over the room.

"And what does your other brother do?" Nigel asked, clearly interested but also trying to lighten the mood.

"He's a Boston Detective." Jacen answered.

"That's an honorable job." Frederick said as he took a sip of his whiskey.

"Is he older than you?" Sonica asked, also trying to lift the mood and control the conversation that Casey and Monica were putting a damper on.

"Yes. I'm the youngest."

"Oh, that's so cute; you and Chelsea are both the younger sibling." Ronica said, gleamingly and truly happy.

"Yes, it is quite cute, isn't it?" Onica added, her face clearly belying her words. Chelsea accepted another glass of champagne and prayed to make it through the rest of the weekend.

~~~~~~~~~~~~~~~~~~~~~~~~

Jacen watched as Chelsea walked into the suite they would be sharing and plopped down on the king-size bed. Jacen sat on the other end and looked over at her.

"Well, that was eventful." he said sarcastically. He had no idea who was friend or foe in the Chelsea's array of family. Some were downright rude and cynical, while others appeared friendly. The tension between Chelsea and Monica was very evident.

"I'm sorry about that." She answered with no feeling in her voice.

"What's the deal with you and Monica?" He never saw a sibling so cold to anyone. Sure, Monica didn't seem too pleasant in her attitude toward him, but her disdain for Chelsea was apparent. He was curious as to why? In the years he'd known Chelsea, no one ever had an issue with her. He wondered what happened with her sister. Then, there was her sister's husband, Casey. What was going on with him? He seemed to be happy Chelsea was around and almost shocked that she'd had a boyfriend. He didn't know the extent of Chelsea's dating life, but he learned some time back she had dated a guy named Rodney. Jacen knew of him. He was a regular at the diner and worked in advertising, even helped his friend Donovan a few times.

"She hates me, I told you." She answered, leaning back on the bed staring at the ceiling with her hands resting on her stomach.

"I'm sure there's a story behind that." She nodded but didn't say anything. He could tell it bothered her, although she was trying to hide it. Something was wrong, but as much as he wanted to pry, he knew he wouldn't. Or at least not right now. Laying back on the bed, choosing the same posture as her, he looked over at Chelsea. It took a few minutes, but she looked over at him and their eyes connected.

"What time is the rehearsal dinner?" he asked.

"We have a couple of hours?"

"Formal or informal?"

"Informal, thank God. Sonica is not as traditional as Ronica...or Monica?"

"Ronica does seem a little stylish." He remembered seeing her in the latest fashion swimsuit after removing her coverup, saying she wanted to swim.

"Yes, Ronica is all about fashion. That's how she met Garrett."

"Garrett's into fashion." He asked.

"His family is. They sponsor and promote brands on models for commercials, magazines, and events."

"Ronica was a model?"

"No, Ronica loves clothes and styling. Although out of all of them, she has the best body for it." She paused before saying. "Three sides of the pyramid."

"What do you mean?"

"Ronica has the body, Sonica has the brain, and Monica has the heart."

"Monica has a heart. You could have fooled me." He laughed.

"Who knew, huh." She said, sharing a laugh with him.

"What about you?" She quirked a brow at him.

"Me? What do you mean?"

"What part of the pyramid are you?" she turned to look back at the ceiling.

"I'm the base, the stain they want no one to see." Jacen didn't say anything for a while. He didn't like that she saw herself that way. Outside of Monica and maybe some side comments by Onica, her father and other two sisters seem happy she was around.

"You're not a stain, Chelsea. Trust me, they see you." She looked back over at him. The light cascading down on her from the window in the room hit her face at an angle where her light brown eyes seem to reflect a speck of gold. She was beautiful. He wondered why he never saw Chelsea like this before. Why hadn't he taken the time to study her features? She had the same full cheeks as her father, her small well-cut nose he assumed was from her mother, as her sister's slender noses resembled their fathers. Her soft jawline connected to her straight oval chin and her sweetly curved lips covered by a smooth pink gloss she applied right before they stepped out of the limo. Taking his hand, he gently placed a piece of her hair behind her ear. The instinct to kiss her slowly rose inside of him. Jacen wanted to feel her soft lips pressed against his own. His phone vibrated in his pockets, interrupting his thoughts. Closing his eyes in annoyance at the interruption, he took his phone from his pants and checked the screen. His brother Jerome was calling him.

"Hey Rome, What's up?"

"Not sure little brother. My wife is not too happy about you leaving the city all of a sudden without telling her." He almost rolled her eyes. Shayna was way too controlling at times.

"Tell her I'll be back for the first photoshoot and not to worry her pretty little head. Nothing wrong with wanting a quick mini-vacation before the madness starts."

"I thought you were looking forward to this?"

"I was. I mean, I am. The timing is just not as convenient as I would like." Jacen further explained to his brother about the investor he thought he'd acquire backing out.

"Do you need a silent partner?"

"Yes."

"Maybe, you should talk to dad."

"Dad? Since when does he know investors?" He heard Jerome chuckling through the phone.

"You've heard of Donald Blake, right?"

"The Billionaire from Houston?" Jacen asked, standing up from the bed.

"That's the one."

"Dad knows him?"

"Shocking right, but yes." It was beyond shocking. His dad was a retired firefighter, well known, and respected in the community. He'd met several political and elite figures in Massachusetts, but a billionaire from Texas? How did that happen?

"Anyway, when you get back, you might want to have a talk with him." Jerome continued saying.

"Yes, I'll be sure to do that. Thanks, Rome."

"Don't mention it. Hey, it wouldn't be a coincidence that Chelsea just happens to be out of town this weekend also, would it?" Jacen slowly looked over at Chelsea, still lying on the bed. It seemed for a moment that she'd dozed off.

"Yup, complete coincidence." He heard Jerome groan, clearly not believing him.

"Be careful little brother." He noticed the warning sign in Jerome's voice.

"Always." With that said, he hung up. Walking back over to the bed, his suspicions had been correct; Chelsea had fallen asleep. He wondered if he could steal the kiss he wanted before his brother's call. Jacen shook his head and walked over to where his luggage was placed in the corner of the room. He was a little shocked that he and Chelsea were sharing a suite. However, there was plenty of room. The king-size bed, a full-length sofa alongside a small table, and two chairs all fit comfortably. The different themed decor he noticed downstairs extended upstairs also. The only difference was the rooms upstairs were themed to movies or comics. The room he and Chelsea were in held the theme of Dick Tracy, the detective. He hadn't been a fan of the show, but his father had been. Yellow, black, and specks of red coloring around created a lovely tribute to the 1990s version of the show, then the original 1945 series. Placing his luggage on the couch, he figured he'd take a quick shower and change before the rehearsal dinner. From the advice of his brother and his two friends, getting ready before a woman was always the best route. He looked over Chelsea again, noticing the slight rise and fall of her chest as she slept, and fought down his desire to kiss her once again. Trying to dismiss his thoughts, he walked into the bathroom and turned on the shower. Stepping in after undressing, he allowed the water to wash over him while picturing Chelsea looking so soft and sweet as she slept. What was happening to him? They hadn't been away from Boston for five hours yet, and he already felt like he might not be able to control his desire for her.

Chapter Eight

Chelsea took in another deep breath; she was pretty sure she would need some type of therapy after this weekend. Seated at the twenty-seater table that included her father and stepmother, Monica and Ronica, with Garrett and Casey. Sonica, her fiancé Nigel and his parents, and a few of his cousins. Taking another sip of her water, she listened as Onica made her over-exaggerated speech at the rehearsal. Forever needing the spotlight. The only other person craving unnecessary attention was Monica. Like mother, like daughter, two peas in a very expensive pod. She felt Jacen take her hand under the table and smile, appreciating his supportive gesture. She took a nap earlier by pure accident. Jacen had woken her up, smelling every bit of the shower he'd taken. She actually regretted not waking up sooner. He was dressed in a grey polo shirt, khaki slacks, and some comfortable-looking men's dress shoes. Chelsea always envied that about men. Their shoes always seemed comfortable. Nothing like the three-inch soft pink heels she wore now. They complimented her sundress alongside her jewelry and other accessories.

But she would definitely need to rub her feet later. Finally, her father stood, cutting into Onica's speech of going down the memory lane of Sonica's birth, her first word, and her first steps.

"I want to thank you all for coming and toast to a full weekend." Everyone raised their glass in salute as Monica stood.

"I just want to make sure everyone knows what we have planned and are expected to attend." After Monica shared the details and answered any questions about the weekend events tomorrow and the schedule for the wedding day, Chelsea excused herself to go to the ladies' room. Once she finished and washed her hands, she heard footsteps in the hall and could see a person by the door. She figured Jacen was coming to check on her, but when she opened the door, leaning against the wall wasn't Jacen, it was Casey. Instantly trying not to flinch, she moved to walk past him, but he blocked her.

"Do you plan on ignoring me this entire weekend, Chelly?" She hated that nickname.

"That's exactly what I planned to do. And my name is Chelsea." She hoped her voice sounded as strong as she needed it to be for him to get the message. She had no intention of interacting with him that weekend.

"You used to like it when I called you that." He said.

"I've always hated it." She admitted. She saw the sting of her words display on his face.

"I used to call you that all the time." Casey stated, taking a step toward her. She took a step back only to hit the wall. Casey placed a hand on the wall beside her head, blocking her from the rest of the hallway.

"Yes, well, that was a long time ago."

"We never discussed it."

"There was nothing to discuss." She said.

"I missed you." He said just above a whisper. She flinched at his words. How dare he say that to her. What happened between them had been so long ago, and clearly, it meant nothing for him to turn around and marry her sister.

"Stop!" She almost shouted. Taking every ounce of strength she had, she pushed him away from her. The force wasn't big enough to make him stumble, but he did drop his arm off the wall and took a step back.

"Please talk to me, Chelsea." Casey pleaded.

"We have nothing to talk about."

"Why am I not surprised?" They both turned to see Monica practically marching down the hall. Casey took another step back.

"You just couldn't wait, could you? Not even twelve hours, and you're already all over my husband."

"I didn't touch him." Chelsea snared. She hated this. It was always like this between them. No matter what, Monica found a way to make it her fault, even when she was the one wronged.

"It's only a matter of time." Monica spurted back.

"Chelsea?" Jacen was now entering the hall, Ronica and Garret following. She instantly turned to walk toward Jacen. Monica grabbed her arm.

"Stay away from my husband." Chelsea snatched away.

"Gladly." She shouted loud enough for everyone to hear. Stalking past Jacen and the others, she ran out the side of the veranda. Chelsea could hear Jacen calling her name, but she didn't stop. She knew any minute tears would fall, and she wouldn't

let them see her cry. She would never let them see
her cry.

~~~~~~~~~~~~~~~~~~~~~~~~~~~~~~~~~

Jacen ran after Chelsea, keeping sight of her
as long as possible before she ran past the boathouse
and onto the wooden pier and stopped. Holding on to
the railing, he could see her gripping it so tight her
knuckles were turning white.

"Chelsea?" She shook her head, not looking at
him, her body slightly hunched toward the railing,
and before he could speak again, he heard a sob. It
was light, almost as if she were trying to hold it in.
What in the world just happened? One minute he was
talking with Garret, and the next, Monica, in a rage,
stomping out of the room. The moment he heard her
yell. He went to see what the issue was. Chelsea was
talking with Casey. What bothered him the most was
Monica's stance and anger toward Chelsea but none
toward her husband. *Stay away from my husband.* He
heard her say. What happened between Chelsea and
Casey? Is that why Chelsea never came home? Why
was she living in Boston alone? He reached out his
hand to gently place it on her shoulder. She shuttered
a bit before looking over at him, and he instantly

wanted to hurt everyone for making her cry. Mascara tears ran down her face that she didn't even try to hide, but what got to him was her eyes, hooded, painful, sorrowful. He took a step forward and pulled her into his arms, and it seemed the floodgates opened, and she cried harder.

"Shhhh. I'm here." He said gently while rubbing her back. He wasn't even entirely sure what was going on. In the last few years that he'd known Chelsea, he'd never seen her sad, let alone crying. She was happy, sweet, shy at times, helpful, and kind. He knew at that moment he'd want to protect her, wanted to always make sure she felt safe, and he never wanted to see her cry again. He felt her stiffen and pulled back slightly as footsteps were heard approaching the pier. She didn't look at him, just wiped her eyes as best she could. When he turned around, he saw Ronica standing behind them.

"Chelsea, are you okay?" She asked nervously. Chelsea didn't even look at her, didn't answer her. She didn't look at him either. Taking deep breaths, she continued staring out into the dark waters rustling lightly against the pier pillars.

Chelsea's face, deep in thought, shone in the moonlight.

"Please don't leave." Ronica continued. "I know Monica's a lot, and trust me, Sonica is giving her an earful at the moment." Chelsea still said nothing. Her back was rigid as she continued to inhale and exhale slowly. She was fighting whatever was torturing her at the moment, and he wished he knew what that was. Whatever demons she was facing, he wanted to fight them for her. He wanted to eliminate everything that ailed her. It was a newfound feeling for him. He never felt protective over any woman, excluding the ones in his family. As Chelsea continued breathing slowly but not speaking, Ronica finally looked over at him, rubbing her protruding belly slowly. He noticed the nervousness in her eyes and the hopelessness that displayed. She really wanted Chelsea to stay.

"Chelsea." He called her name as gently as his voice would allow. She finally looked at him and then slowly over to Ronica.

"I'm not leaving." She said just above a whisper. He heard Ronica exhaled slightly as if she'd been holding her breath, waiting for an answer. She nodded and turned slowly to exit the pier. Looking back over at Chelsea, Jacen extended his hand, hoping she'd take it. She looked down at it for a few seconds before finally placing hers in his. Despite the slightly warm night air, her fingertips felt cool. She looked up at him after watching their hands intertwined.

"I ruined your shirt." She said. The shirt was the least of his concerns.

"I have plenty more." He responded. She nodded and slightly averted her eyes from his. "I would ask if you're alright, but I honestly don't think you are, and I doubt at this moment you'd tell me the truth." He continued.

"I'm sorry." she said, looking down. Jacen ducked his head as best he could to get her eyes to connect with his. His height made that a little uncomfortable, but he wasn't going to complain. She did look up and turn her head to look directly into his eyes. He smiled at her and was grateful when she smiled back and slightly chuckled. The joy in her eyes slowly returned.

"Should we head back?" He asked. She nodded, and together they walked off the pier and back to the house.

~~~~~~~~~~~~~~~~~~~~~~~~~

Jacen allowed Chelsea a few moments to herself once they returned to the room. He knew she wanted to take a bath and relax, so he asked Jasper where the wine cellar was. Jacen wasn't a big drinker, but he'd learned quite a few things about wine in his younger days. An idea at that time he thought would impress Alexia. Her family owned a vineyard.

"Rough night?" Jasper asked. Jacen nodded as Jasper corked a bottle of wine and poured Jacen a glass. Jacen accepted it, inhaled a slight whiff, swirled the wine gently in the glass, and took a sip.

"Are you some sort of wine expert?" Jasper asked.

"I find the process intriguing. I've hosted a few wine tastings at my club."

"Really?" Jacen nodded. "In all my years, I've never had the pleasure of meeting a nightclub owner." Jasper admitted. Jacen smiled, taking another sip. The wine was pretty good.

"How many years have you worked for Frederick Stone?" Jacen asked.

"I actually worked for his uncle as a young boy." Jasper paused as he took a sip from his own glass. "I've known that man almost all of his life. Watched him grow up, build his business, fall in love." Jasper continued.

"Onica?" Jacen questioned. He watched Jasper look into his glass then back to him with a smile.

"No, Rachelle was his first love. His only love." He said.

"He never loved Onica.?" Jacen asked. It seemed strange that the Hollywood producer never fell in love with the woman the bore three of his children.

"Oh, I'm sure he loved Onica for a time. But his heart always belonged to the one he couldn't have."

"Why couldn't he be with her?" Jacen questioned.

"Oh, you know the same old forbidden love between black and white." Jacen's eyebrows furrowed at the tone in Jasper's voice. He said black and white.

"Chelsea's mom?" Jacen asked.

"You pick up quickly, Jacen Turner."

"He knew her before Onica?"

"Yes. He pined after her most of his teenage years." Jacen heard the chuckle in his voice as Jasper recalled Frederick making a fool out of himself trying to gain Rachelle's affections. "She was a lot wiser than him. A lot more understanding of the worldview on their relationship." Jacen nodded, understanding that even now, some people saw a problem with interracial couples.

"So what happened?" Jacen asked, fully engrossed with Jasper's words.

"She knew he wanted to go into movies and make a name for himself in Hollywood. Knew that people at that time wouldn't take him seriously with a black woman at his side, so she tried to leave him."

"I'm guessing Fredrick didn't make it easy for her."

"Oh no, he did the one thing he knew would keep her in his life."

"What was that?" Jacen asked.

"He convinced her to marry him."

"What?"

"Yes. It took lots of convincing too. Even promised to keep things between them a secret, it won her over." Jacen took another sip of his wine. Completely confused by the story now. If Rachelle was Chelsea's mom, then how did Onica come into the picture.

"I see that mind of yours is churning. You're thinking about the timeline, huh?" Jacen nodded.

"Well, that's the kicker. I honestly have gaps in my story too." Jasper admitted.

"Did he ever divorce her?"

"No, they stayed married until she died." Jasper answered.

"When did she die?" Jacen asked.

"A couple of years after Chelsea was born. She couldn't have been more than three years old when Fredrick brought her home."

"Did Onica know about Rachelle?"

"No, not until Fredrick walked home with Chelsea in his arms." Jacen's eyes blanched at that thought.

"I'm sure that didn't go over well."

"You nailed it. Onica was adamant about him getting rid of her. It was the first time I ever saw Fredrick lose his temper, which shocked the crap out of Onica. Everything sort of spilled out all at once in his anger. Frederick and Onica had decided to call it quits almost four years prior. Onica at the time was unaware of being pregnant with Monica, Frederick was ready to leave Hollywood behind and finally have a life with Rachelle. Neither one of them realized Monica standing by the door and hearing it all. She'd never heard her parents fight before that night." Jasper finished off the last of his wine when he finished speaking.

"Is that why Monica seems to hate Chelsea?"

"Yes." Jasper answered flatly.

"I thought it might have something to do with Casey."

"That just added fuel to the already blazing fire." Jasper said.

"What happened between Casey and Chelsea?" Jacen asked. Jasper sighed.

"The same thing that always happens between a young boy choosing between his heart and his family's wishes."

"He loved her." Jacen stated, more than questioned.

"Still does." Jasper admitted. Although Jacen could have guessed as much, hearing the words didn't sit right with him.

"Did Chelsea love him?" Jacen asked, looking into his wine glass. He didn't want to admit to himself that the thought of Chelsea loving another man bothered him.

"I'm sure she did. Puppy love is what we call it, but Monica also did, and Onica saw to it that she got him." Jacen rested back in his chair, taking in all that Jasper had shared.

"I'm not too sure of what to do with the information you've shared with me, Jasper."

"You seem like the type to stick around Jacen Turner. Chelsea needs someone like you in her life." Jasper admitted.

"I hope you're right." Jacen said, taking the last sip and handing his empty wine glass to Jasper.

Chapter Nine

Chelsea sipped her mimosa in her chair, watching as Sonica unwrapped gifts. The bridal shower brunch was held at the Masterson Country Club in Pensacola. The room was decorated in white lace with hints of silver throughout. Even the flute she held was covered in lace, and a silver lining etched the bottom and tip of the glass. Monica practically ignored her, which was fine by Chelsea. After last night's embarrassing moment with Casey, and her inability to keep her emotions in check, she was thankful no one brought it up, and Monica left her alone. Usually, things between the three of them didn't affect her as they had last night. She really wasn't sure why she thought bringing a boyfriend home would make things different. Wishing just once, she could avoid the drama, the constant feeling of being the outcast and just enjoy her time with her father.

A few claps around the room brought Chelsea back to the present. Sonica thanked everyone for her gifts, adding a little touch of her happiness to marrying Nigel in her speech, and instructed everyone to join her in the motorcade. The real partying was about to begin. Chelsea finished off the rest of her drink and grabbed her bag next to her. Onica made it very clear they would not be returning to the house before late tonight. A spa visit, a few stops to some shops, and nightlife in Pensacola for the bachelorette party awaiting them. Ronica wasn't staying the entire day, frustrated she couldn't drink because she was pregnant and claiming she'd be too tired to party. As she entered the motorcade, Chelsea felt her phone vibrate. Taking her seat, she noticed a text from Ashiree and a missed text from Jacen asking how she was doing. She quickly responded to Ashiree leaving out last night's fiasco and then responded to Jacen.

I'm doing okay, we're in the motorcade now. How are you?

I'm good, you had me worried for a minute, you didn't wake me before you left.

I know, sorry, Onica was freaking out about us being late.

It's cool. We're about to head out on the boat. I'm not sure if my phone will have a signal.

Probably not but have fun, don't let the guys peer pressure you :)

I have three older brothers, I think I can handle myself.

I'm sure you can. I'll see you later.

Okay.

~~~~~~~~~~~~~~~~~~~~~~~~~~~~~~~~

"Texting Chelsea?" Garret asked as Jacen put his phone back in his pocket.

"Yes, I'm checking on her."

That's good; she needs someone like you." Jacen eyed him skeptically. Jasper had said the same thing.

"I've just been around for a few years. Not as long as Casey, but long enough to know Chelsea can be a loner. I'm not close to my family other than us doing business together, but Chelsea's always had that air about her. Ronica talks about her all the time. Says she wishes she'd been more of a sister to her." Jacen nodded, not wanting to get into the family drama today. After his conversation with Jasper last night, he wasn't sure how to feel about Chelsea's family. It was a lot to take in. Returning to their room from the wine cellar, he watched Chelsea sleep for a while. Her slow intakes of breath indicated she was sleeping peacefully, but her face was etched with lines of worry, and her eyes fluttered slightly every few seconds. He took the settee across from her to sleep, not daring to sleep beside her. He didn't want to fight the urge to hold her, and he didn't want to wake her up. He was becoming very protective of Chelsea, a feeling unfamiliar to him. And one he wasn't sure how to handle.

"You boys ready for a day you'll never forget." Nigel and two other men stepped on the boat. The shortest one looked very much like a Ken barbie doll.

"We're not getting into any mischief today Tommie." Garrett said sternly.

"Don't be such a stiff neck, Garrett. Who's the new guy?" the man named Tommie said while reaching into the cooler to grab a beer. He tossed it to the other man standing beside Nigel and reached back into the cooler.

"Chelsea's boyfriend." Garrett answered. Tommie whipped his head up so quickly Jacen thought it might pop off. The other man was now staring at him too.

"Our Chelsea?" Tommie asked.

"How many Chelsea's do you know? Yes, our Chelsea." Garrett answered. The two men looked at each other and then back to him and Garret.

"Does Casey know?" The other man asked in a very concerned voice. Jacen quirked a brow and felt Garrett stiffen next to him.

"I'm guessing he does." Tommie said, cracking open his beer. "That explains his pounding on the gym bag this morning." Tommie continued taking a swig of his beer. Garrett looked over at Jacen with an apologetic look.

"I'm Steven Worthington, Casey's older brother." The third man said, stepping over to shake Jacen's hand. Jacen reached up to accept it.

"Jacen Turner."

"It's nice to meet you. This idiot right here is Tommie, the youngest, as you can tell by his lack of tack."

"Someone has to bring life into that dull world of yours, oh ancient one." Tommie said, clamping his arm around Steven's neck, clearly teasing him. Nigel chuckled a little, and Tommie and Steven both sat and made small talk until Casey, along with Fredrick and Jasper, stepped onto the deck. With Jasper at the helm, they set sail.

The next two hours were pure bliss. Standing at the front of the upper deck balcony, Jacen enjoyed the breeze and the midday sun. Open water, the horizon in front of them, made him definitely consider getting a boat after this trip.

"I truly love this scenery." Jacen heard Frederick say as he came to stand alongside him with a glass of scotch in his hand.

"It's quite a scene." he responded, not taking his eyes off the water. Silence hung between them before either of them spoke.

"How long have you known my daughter Jacen Turner?" Jacen smirked a little. He honestly hadn't considered having a conversation with Chelsea's father before coming with her.

"Almost eight years, sir."

"Would you say you two are well acquainted?" Jacen's brow deepened. He hoped Fredrick Stone was not asking him what he thought he was.

"My relationship with Chelsea is new, and we're taking things slow." Frederick seemed to understand his answer and took a slow sip from his glass.

"Jasper told me he spoke with you last night." Jacen nodded.

"He's taken a liking to you. Not to mention Garret's continual praises of your family." Frederick continued. Jacen smiled.

"Do you mind if I ask what your father does?" Fredrick inquired.

"He's a retired fireman." Jacen told Fredrick.

"All around good American man. I thought about being a fireman as a child."

"What happened?"

"I found out I could make a lot more money playing them in films." Fredrick answered. They both shared a laugh.

"That seems to have worked out well for you." Jacen stated.

"Yes, I can agree it did." Jasper was docking the boat near a pier close to South Miami.

"Are you gentlemen ready for a night on the town?" Tommie interrupted, walking up with the other guys in tow. Throwing his arm around Fredricks's shoulders.

"Translation...Strip club." Garrett added.

"Yes! Since Nigel is the completely faithful type, I feel it is my responsibility to partake in everything he doesn't."

"You'll have to enjoy whatever you partake in without me, but you boys have fun." Frederick said, extracting himself from under Tommie's arm.

"All, come on old man. I promise not to tell Onica we paid to get you a lap dance." Tommie teased. Jacen chuckled, and so did the others.

"I would hope not. She'd be very upset to know she missed the action." Frederick said, walking off, leaving Tommie stunned, while Nigel threw his head back and laughed.

~~~~~~~~~~~~~~~~~~~~~~~~~

Chelsea thanked Jacen as he helped zip up the back of her dress. She tried not to notice the slight similarities in their attire. Her half sleeve, knee-length burgundy dress matched well with Jacen's tux. His tie and cloth both matched her dress almost perfectly. She turned to face him.

"Thank you for doing this." She said earnestly. She'd wanted to hope for the best this weekend and felt horrible to have brought Jacen into the mess she had going on with her family. But after today, it would all be over, and they would return to Boston.

"It's no problem." Jacen said in response while looking down at her. He really was a good-looking man. She could easily steal glances at him without his knowledge when things were busy at the diner or the club. But now, in the close proximity that they were, she could admit, she could stare at him all day.

"Do I look alright?" He asked.

"You look perfect." She whispered and blinked as she realized what she said. Jacen smiled almost in a chuckle.

"I mean…" Chelsea began trying to recover from the previous blubber.

"What do you mean, Chelsea?" He closed the short distance between, and the scent of him wrapped its way around her nostrils. She stared into his eyes, completely allured by his sharp gaze. She watched his eyes slightly avert to her lips, then connect back with hers. Before she could ponder on how many times she'd dreamed of kissing him, he lowered his head, and arched her neck as his lips slowly touched

~ 117 ~

hers. Whatever she thought a kiss with him would be like was utterly shot as he probed open her mouth, exploring every inch with his tongue. Jacen Turner was making love to her mouth and kissing her senseless. Her arms, of their own free will, slowly wrapped around his neck, holding him to her. She felt his arms wrap around her waist, pulling her closer as he turned his head, devouring her mouth from a different angle. She heard Jacen slowly groan, felt his body as he brought her even closer to him.

"Hey, you lovebirds. The limo leaves in ten minutes." Chelsea heard Lorelai say with a slight knock on their room door. Their kiss ended, but neither of them backed away.

"We should probably get going." Chelsea managed to say. Slowly removing her arms from his neck. The air sizzled around them, and the aftermath of their kiss still vibrated through her body.

"Yes, we should." Jacen said but didn't pull away or loosen his embrace on her. Chelsea stared into his dark brown eyes, filled with heat and desire. She could hear the erratic heartbeat in her chest. The second knock on the door seemed to finally break the spell, and Jacen released her and stepped back.

"Are you ready?" He asked. She nodded, grabbed her wrap, and together they headed out of their room.

~~~~~~~~~~~~~~~~~~~~~~~~~~~

Jacen grabbed his second glass of champagne as he watched Chelsea take a few pictures with Sonica. The wedding was small. With a few hundred guests. A complete contrast to his best friend's wedding a few months ago. He smiled, thinking about Trent and Kaitlyn's wedding. Trent's mother went all out, inviting over three thousand guests for the nuptials of her only son. Jacen was sure Constance went slightly overboard with Trent since, to her utter dismay, Trent's sister Danyelle had eloped. Taking a drink from his flute, he watched Chelsea smile once again for a photo. This time she was joined by both Ronica and Monica. She and Monica were on opposite sides of the bride, and although it seemed no words were exchanged, the tension between them was evident. After posing for another photo, she made her way over to where he sat.

"How are you holding up?" He asked as she gracefully took her seat next to him.

"I'm alright. So far, so good." He nodded at her answer and chose not to pry. Honestly, he was just trying to wrap his mind around the kiss they shared earlier. Whatever thoughts he had of what that kiss would be like, failed to compare to what he experienced. He rested back in his chair and watched Chelsea as she watched a few children dance on the dancefloor. He was seeing her in a new light. She was like a gem that had been hiding in broad daylight, now surfaced. He was attracted to Chelsea. She was beautiful, of course, there was no doubt about that, but why hadn't he seen her, like really seen her. She looked over at him and seemed surprised to find he was already looking at her.

"Are you alright?" She asked slight concern etched in her eyes.

"I'm fine, actually better than fine."

"I'm surprised you are not checking on the diner or club every five minutes." She teased. He half-smiled. He spent the majority of his time back home working.

"I guess I should thank you for the getaway."

"I don't know about that. I'm sure it would have been a little less drama in Boston." Chelsea responded.

"Maybe, but the club has its moments of drama." he responded. They shared a slight smirk between them, remembering his bouncers intervening with a few rowdy nightclubbers a few times.

"Thank you for coming with me, Jacen." He heard the sincerity in her voice. Despite the tension with her family, he honestly wouldn't have wanted to be anywhere else. He almost thought to say that to her but thought better of it.

"You can make it up to me." He said, placing his champagne flute on the table.

"Oh really? And how might I do that?"

"How about a dance?" He offered while standing and extending his hand. She smiled shyly, and he led her over to the dance floor. Several other couples, including the bride and the groom, were all dancing. Slowly taking her in his arms, Jacen couldn't help but look down into her light brown eyes. Chelsea was looking directly back up at him, and he wondered what she thought.

"I have a confession to make?" Jacen stated.

"What's that?" she asked.

"I can't get our kiss earlier off my mind." he admitted. He watched Chelsea slightly avert her eyes, then swallow slowly, before looking back up to him.

"Jacen, I…"

"Do you mind if I cut in?" They both turned to see Casey standing next to them. Jacen's body instantly stiffened, and so had Chelsea's. Hadn't his wife practically threatened Chelsea to stay away from her husband, and now Casey boldly, with everyone watching, just asked to interrupt their dance. Not wanting to cause a scene and disrespect the bride or groom with his thoughts, Jacen looked down at Chelsea.

"Chelsea?" he asked, giving her the option. There were some things in her past with Casey, and although Jasper shared a little light on it, Jacen felt it was a lot more.

"I don't think that's a good idea." Chelsea answered. Jacen was proud of her, but then worry began to settle as she stepped from his arms and turned to leave the dancefloor. Jacen looked over at Casey annoyingly, then shook his head. He followed

Chelsea, seeing that she was not only leaving the dancefloor but also leaving the ballroom.

Chapter Ten

Chelsea did her best no to run from the ballroom. Why had Casey interrupted her dance with Jacen? It didn't take but a quick second for her to see others in the ballroom staring at them, staring at her. She could feel Monica's glare and the challenge in her eyes if she accepted the dance. Knowing the type of scene Monica wouldn't hesitate to display if she danced with Casey. Not that she wanted to. She was in a perfect state of euphoria, hearing Jacen admit that he couldn't forget their kiss. Acknowledging for the first time, that kissing a man sent more than tingles down her body. It shocked her to her core.

"Chelsea, wait." She halted her retreat. Her mind going back to the moment on the dance floor. Why had she brought him here? Why did she get Jacen into this mess?

"I'm sorry." She said sincerely, unable to meet his gaze.

"Chelsea, you have nothing to be sorry for."

"Don't I? Look at the mess I've brought you into."

"Every family has their drama. Or exes that can't let go." She met his eyes with a gasp. He knew. She'd done her best to hide any reaction to Casey. She honestly hadn't thought Casey would be so bold to seek her out.

"You shouldn't have to be subject to it."

"I'm alright as long as you are. I can't imagine you handling this alone." She smiled slightly. She couldn't imagine it either.

"I do appreciate you being here."

"I wouldn't want to be anywhere else, Chelsea." He said with an expression she couldn't read. She wondered if he knew the meaning of his words to her. She couldn't help but smile. Looking into his dark brown eyes, seeing the truth in them. "Are you ready to go back in?"

"No." she said earnestly. "But I don't want to ruin Sonica's day. She doesn't deserve that. No bride does." Jacen nodded in understanding.

"Then let's go back in. We'll tackle it together." He said and extended his arm. She gladly accepted it and took a deep breath.

"You're kind of perfect, you know that Jacen Turner." She said teasingly as they walked back toward the ballroom.

"You're kind of beautiful, you know that Chelsea Stone?" He countered. She nearly lost her footings at his words. He wasn't smiling or displayed any hint of teasing in his gaze on her. She smiled shyly and allowed him to lead her back into the ballroom.

~~~~~~~~~~~~~~~~~~~~~~~~

Chelsea took in her father's scent as she hugged him goodbye. She hated goodbyes, but she longed to get back to her life in Boston. The weekend events, though joyous for Sonica, took a toll on her. Monica and Casey were not in the mini crowd standing in front of the house to see her and Jacen off.

"Try and not stay away so long this time Chel Bell." She smiled at her father's request and nodded. They both knew she wouldn't be coming back any time soon. This had been their routine for so many years. As her father released her, he took a step back and shifted toward Jacen.

"It was a pleasure to meet you, Jacen Turner." Fredrick said, extending his hand. Jacen accepted.

"You also, Mr. Stone."

"Be sure to take care of my little girl." Chelsea heard her father say and noted the love in his voice as he spoke to Jacen.

"I will." They said their final goodbyes to Lorelai, Garret, and Ronica as Jasper finished putting the luggage in the trunk.

"My baby shower is in a couple of months. I want you to come." Ronica stated. Chelsea did her best to hide the shock on her face. Outside of Ronica's wedding, she and Ronica never kept in contact.

"I'd like that." Chelsea answered sincerely. Ronica smiled and hugged her, wishing her a safe trip as she and Jacen entered the back of the limo. Chelsea breathed a side of relief as Jasper began driving the limo away from her father's mansion. She didn't look back, didn't watch as the mansion faded away in the background, didn't see the man in the upper window watching her pull away.

~~~~~~~~~~~~~~~~~~~~

Casey Worthington watched as the limo pulled away. He hadn't expected Chelsea to come. He hadn't seen her in six years, not since Ronica and Garrett had gotten married. She had completely ignored him, and he allowed it. Knowing Monica would blow a head gasket if he made any effort to reach out to her. Casey assumed Chelsea was still upset with him for marrying Monica, but what could he do? He'd made a terrible mistake.

"I'm guessing Chelsea's gone." Casey didn't have to turn around to acknowledge his brother Tommie's words. Casey had no intention of discussing the obvious with Tommie.

"Where did you sneak off to last night?" He questioned.

"Believe it or not, I finally got Lorelai to open up to me." Casey nodded but continue to watch the limo until it was out of his sight.

"You might not want to stare out that window too much longer. I'd hate for Monica to catch you." Tommie said with a chuckle. Everyone knew his wife was a pill, but at this moment, he could care less. She had confronted him about approaching Chelsea for a dance. Generally, in situations or conversations about

Chelsea, he stayed clear of Monica. Her obvious disdain and jealousy of Chelsea were always evident. He didn't know why but Chelsea's attitude toward him bothered him. He thought he could have a moment to talk with her at the rehearsal dinner. He tried lightening the mood with some teasing and a little bit of flirting. But Monica showed up, in rare form, as usual, yelling at Chelsea. He'd spent most of the night restless and unable to sleep. After a few hours, Casey gave up trying and headed to the gym. He wasn't made to lift weights, but he was a man that loved to box. Hours flew by, and he pounded the bag, trying to exhaust himself until Steven walked into the gym, reminding him of Nigel's bachelor party.

He'd tried to speak to her again at the reception, but Chelsea turned him down and the look that her boyfriend gave him, made Casey want to hate him. But with Garrett's incessant need to sing Jacen's praise or, more so, the praises of his brothers, it was hard to. Casey, himself, had worked a few times with Jacen's older brother Justin, and Jacen seemed like a good guy, just what Chelsea needed.

~~~~~~~~~~~~~~~~~~~~~~~

Jacen walked Chelsea to the door of her brownstone and helped her with her luggage.

"Thank you, Jacen, but you didn't have to carry my suitcase."

"What kind of boyfriend would I be if I let you carry your own suitcase in the house?" He said as he placed the suitcase down in her foyer.

"I think you've already proved how good of a boyfriend you can be over the weekend. Thank you for everything." She said, honestly.

"Stop thanking me. I told you, I wouldn't have wanted to be anywhere else." and he meant it. Jacen took a step toward her, loving how she arched her neck to look up at him. He wanted to kiss her. The entire plane ride back to Boston Chelsea had slept on his shoulder. He'd fought every instinct in his body not to press his lips to hers. But he knew she was tired. The weekend with her family put a lot of stress on her. Before he was able to act on his desire, his phone vibrated in his pocket. Slightly groaning as he pulled away and he checked his phone.

"Problem at the club?" He heard Chelsea ask as he responded to a text from one of his bouncers and his club manager.

"Nothing too major, but I do need to go." He said, looking down at her and regretting having to leaving.

"Well, I made it home safe and sound, so it's fine." Chelsea responded. He smiled, glad she was understanding. Anytime something went on with the club or the diner, he was prompt in getting there.

"We have a photoshoot in a couple of days." He said, prolonging the inevitable.

"Yes, Shayna emailed me the itinerary."

"Are you still okay with our arrangement?"

"Of course, I won't go back now. Especially after this weekend." She said with a hint of sarcasm in her voice. He nodded and eventually allowed himself to open the front door.

"I'll call you tomorrow." He said, settling for kissing her cheek before heading out to his car.

~~~~~~~~~~~~~~~~~~~~~~~~~

Chelsea sighed as she read through the final copy of the romance novel she was editing. There was nothing like a good happily ever after. She didn't care how they came as long as the hero and heroine ended up together and very much in love. It was close to two a.m. she realized and stood from her reading chair on her second floor living space. The Brownstown, her aunt, left her was way too big for any one person. Her aunt always dreamed of having a big family, but she'd never married and couldn't have children. She told Chelsea that she was the closest thing she'd have to having her own child. And it was an honor to take care of her. Chelsea recalled the times her aunt had come to visit her after her mother died. It didn't seem like her aunt and father got along, and her aunt truly hated Onica. As a child, she didn't understand it, and wanted everyone to love each other and get along. It was why she tried so hard to get Monica to like her. Ronica and Sonica being older, didn't play with them as much. Monica would play tricks on her, causing her to either get in trouble or get hurt. As they got older, Monica's antics were more on the dangerous side. She'd burned Chelsea with a curling iron while trying to curl her doll's hair. Chelsea lied for her, claiming it was an accident, hoping to gain Monica's trust. It hadn't worked. At ten years old, she'd pushed Chelsea off the monkey bars at the park, locked her in one of the closets, and cut off all Chelsea's hair. The last and final straw was when she was thirteen, Monica had replaced her body lotion with some itching powder that caused an allergic reaction to Chelsea's skin, and she was hospitalized for three days. Her aunt had flown down to see her in the hospital. She didn't witness the conversation between her aunt and her father, but when she left the hospital, she moved to Boston and hadn't returned to her father's home until she turned eighteen.

Heading over to her computer, she spent a few hours entering all her edits, formations, and suggestions to the author. It was almost six in the morning before she finally showered and settled into bed. She was grateful her aunt invested in blackout shades for her bedroom. As a night nurse, her aunt slept most days and completely blocking out the sunlight helped. Setting her alarm on her phone, she snuggled underneath her covers, allowing the beautiful love story she'd read to infiltrate her thoughts. She let the replaying story cast her into a deep sleep with a smile on her face, replacing the main character with a very handsome nightclub owner.

~~~~~~~~~~~~~~~~~~~~~~~~~~~

Jacen parked his SUV in front of his childhood home and cut the engine. Exiting his car, Jacen looked around the neighborhood. Not much changed since he was a young boy. The street still housed many people around the age of his parents or their children. Walking up the driveway, he knocked before opening the door announcing his presence. His mother was pleased to greet him and informed him that his father was in his study. Walking into his father's study, Justin Turner Sr. was sitting at his desk with a paper in his hand and glasses on his face.

"Jacen is so good to see you." He said, hearing Jacen entering the room.

"Hey dad, how are you doing today?" Jacen asked. His father responded that he was doing well for an old man. Jacen chuckled and took a seat in front of the desk. He gave his father a quick update on the nightclub and diner when he asked. It helped Jacen lead into the question about an investor.

"Dad, can I ask you a question?"

"Sure, son, what is it?" Justin Sr. asked, removing her glasses from his face.

"Jerome mentioned you might know Donald Blake?" Justin Sr. nodded with a smile.

"Yes, Donald and I go back a few years."
Jacen listened as his father gave him the back story of
meeting Donald Blake.

"Wow. How's his family now?" Jacen asked.
He watched as a solemn look displayed on his face.

"All that's left is him and his grandchildren."
His father answered.

"That's a lot of tragedy." Jacen responded in
mild shock.

"It is, but why the sudden interest in Donald?"
Jacen rubbed the back of his neck and sat up a little
in his chair.

"I'm looking for an investor. I've found a
second location for the club, but none of the investors
I've come up with are working out. I was just
wondering if you think he would be interested." Jacen
asked nervously.

"Donald is involved in so much." Justin Sr.
said with a chuckle. "The last time I spoke with him,
he was in negotiations for some pharmaceutical
company in Houston."

"Do you think you can get me in contact with
him?" Jacen asked hopefully.

"I'll see what I can do. Give me a couple days."

"Thanks, dad." Jacen said with slight relief. He spent more minutes with his father before politely excusing himself after receiving a call about an issue at the diner. He quickly headed toward the kitchen to kiss his mother before he left.

Chapter Eleven

"Do you have any idea how much these cost?" Chelsea heard as she walked over to a lady standing over the new waitress. Chelsea could see the waitress's hand slightly shaking as she picked up the items that fell off her tray.

"I demand to speak to Jacen this instant." The woman practically shouted.

"He isn't here at the moment; maybe I can help you." Chelsea says once she reached the table. The woman turned around and Chelsea was almost taken back to see Lauren Ellis staring at her.

"How can you help me? You don't even technically work here?" Chelsea couldn't argue with that. The regular manager had to leave to pick up her son when his school called to say he was sick. It was only an hour before Jacen was due to come in, so Chelsea volunteered to stand in.

"I'm filling in for Heidi."

"You can't help me. Where is Jacen?" Lauren demanded.

"Again, he isn't here. Now I can make arrangements to have the cook remake your meal, and have the bill is taken care of."

"I want her fired." Lauren shouted.

"Nobody is getting fired." Chelsea almost stiffened as she heard Jacen's voice behind her. Turning slowly, she watched as he approached. The lining of his jaw was tight with irritation. "What are you doing here, Lauren?" He asked. Lauren's face softened as she looked over Jacen.

"I wanted to see you." She answered softly.

"And you thought being rude and causing a scene in my diner would make me happy to see you."

"These are three-thousand-dollar boots that she ruined." Lauren ranted. Chelsea looked down at Lauren's boots and frowned. If she spent that much money on knockoffs, Chelsea felt terrible for her. She wasn't big on fashion, but you couldn't grow up with the world's most renowned supermodel as your stepmother and not know a thing or two about particular designers.

"I'll pay for the boots." Jacen said flatly. Chelsea's head wiped up in shock. The boots weren't even authentic.

"I'd rather you fire her." Lauren says, pointing at the waitress. Chelsea almost spoke up, but Jacen beat her to the punch.

"That won't be happening." Jacen answered, folding his arms in front of him. Chelsea tried not to stare at how the jacket tightened around his arms, showing just how muscled they were. Lauren must have noticed the same because she took a step toward Jacen.

"Can we talk in private?" She asked.

"That won't be happening either. And after today, I'll have to ask you not to come back." Chelsea watched Lauren's eyes widened in shock and embarrassment as she took a step back.

"You can't be serious."

"I'm very serious. You came into my diner, caused a scene, and insulted my staff." Jacen turned his head and nodded to the bouncer for the club, Evan, to escort Lauren from the diner. She didn't go quietly and pleaded for Jacen to speak with her. Jacen ignored her, apologized to the customers in the diner, and compensated everyone's meal for the inconvenience. Chelsea couldn't imagine what that would cost him.

"I'm really sorry, Mr. Turner." The waitress finally said. Chelsea's heart almost broke for her. She was on the brink of tears.

"Don't worry about it. I'm sure it was a mistake. Are you hurt?" She shook her head and headed back behind the counter to discard the items on her tray and grab the next table's meal.

"Thank you for not yelling at her." Chelsea said.

"Do I normally yell?" He asked, puzzled.

"No, but you could have scolded her?"

"It was a mistake, and Lauren is not the most pleasant person to be around." Chelsea nodded but didn't voice her opinion.

"What are you doing here? Where's Heidi?" he asked with genuine curiosity.

"Little Sammy got sick at school, and she had to leave. I was actually already on my way here."

"I'm starting to think this place is your second home." He teased.

"What can I say? I like it here." She admitted, causing his smile to grow wider.

"I need to run to my office. Can you continue holding down the fort?"

"Maybe, do you expect any other ex-girlfriends to come and stir up trouble?" Jacen belted out a laugh.

"Oh, I hope not, but if so, I'm sure my current girlfriend can handle it." He whispered.

"You think so, huh?" She said teasingly.

"I'm sure she can. She is tougher than she seems." He said, winking at her before he headed to the back of the diner and down the stairs to his office.

~~~~~~~~~~~~~~~~~~~~~~~~~~

Lauren slammed her purse on the passenger seat as she sat in her car. Totally embarrassed and frustrated at Jacen's treatment of her, not to mention the silly waitress that spilled an entire tray of food, splatting all of its content over her new boots. At least Jacen said he would replace them; that thought brought her some comfort. Maybe he really did care. She knew she'd miscalculated her steps when she'd spoken to his mother about potentially helping plan their wedding. She and Jacen hadn't dated long, but she knew he was the one for her. She deserved to be the next Turner wife. The photo shooting for the Charity Calendar was about to begin. No woman's name had been announced yet as his date, and Lauren saw no reason for Jacen to do it alone. That had been her only reason for trying to speak with him today. She was surprised to find out he had been out of town. Jacen never took weekends off or left the state for a weekend event. She reached over to grab her purse and retrieve her cell phone. She texted him, apologizing and praying he would respond so they could move on, and hopefully, him agreeing to let her be his date for the calendar.

~~~~~~~~~~~~~~~~~~~~~~

Jacen rubbed the back of his neck and stretched his muscles. His phone beeped again, and he chose to ignore it. Ever since Lauren was escorted out of his diner, she'd been blowing up his phone, no doubt upset. His thoughts shifted back to Chelsea. Why had Chelsea stayed helping him? He remembered the night more than three months ago at Trent's wedding. It had been hard for him to get coverage at the club that weekend to stand in at Trent's wedding. During the reception, one of his bartenders texted him, informing him of the incident at the club. He remembered regretting that he had to leave the reception early. He'd bumped into Chelsea and Ashiree, and Chelsea had offered their services, which Ashiree wasn't too happy about. They had been a godsend for him that night. Working until almost sunrise. Jacen later hired Heidi for diner and another waitress for the bar. After a few weeks, he was fully staffed and seeing Chelsea became a norm, but he never asked her why she stayed and helped. She and Heidi got along well, but then again, Chelsea got along with everyone.

He took a breath and remembered his time with her family. They hadn't discussed anything since returning to Boston, and Jacen wanted to know more about her and her family, not to mention Casey. He felt slightly uncomfortable how he seemed to keep his eyes constantly on Chelsea, despite his wife shooting daggers at him with her eyes. There was definitely history there and hurt. He'd seen Chelsea completely break down at the confrontation with Monica while in Pensacola. At the time, he'd wanted to help her get through the weekend. But now, he wanted to know more about his pretend girlfriend. Hearing the chime on his phone yet again, he thought of blocking Laurens's number, but when he grabbed his phone to look at the message coming through, it wasn't Lauren's number. It was Trent's. Deciding to respond, he opened the text to Trent, inviting him to his home. The team had an off week coming up, and whenever Trent had time, they got together for at least one night. He confirmed the time and made a mental note.

~~~~~~~~~~~~~~~~~~~~~~~~~~

"Lauren's back on the rant again." Ashiree announced from her room.

"What are you talking about?" Chelsea said, while straightening the towels in Ashiree's bathroom. Ashiree came to stand in the doorway a few seconds later. Her phone in her hand.

"Someone's upset set about a certain Turner brother having his bouncer escort her out of the diner."

"What?" Chelsea exclaimed, walking over as Ashiree turned the phone toward her. Clear and in rare form, Lauren was spurting comments on her social media, claiming to be the victimized ex-girlfriend.

"They barely dated." Chelsea said.

"True, but when did this happen?"

"They the other day when Lauren yelled at the new waitress for ruining her new boots. She made such a scene and completely embarrassed her." Chelsea said, explaining what took place after Jacen arrived.

"Now you see why I choose not to like her." Ashiree said, then looked past Chelsea. "I have no idea why you bother to do that." Noting the towel set, Chelsea carefully placed on the towel rack.

"I don't understand why you still have boxes unpacked in your closet." Chelsea countered. Ashiree rolled her eyes, walked over into her small living area, and plopped down on her couch.

"What difference does it make. I'll probably be moving shortly."

"Moving where?" Chelsea asked.

"Who knows." Ashiree said with a shrug, then added. "You know I'm not comfortable staying in one place too long." Chelsea didn't respond but knew it was true. Ashiree moved around a lot, seeming to reflect her younger years of bouncing from foster home to foster home. Chelsea worried about her, but she didn't voice her concern.

"So, when are you and Jacen going on an official date?" Chelsea smiled at Ashiree probing. She and Jacen had not been on an official date. After returning from Florida, their schedules seem to clash, and she hadn't spent that much time at the diner in the last week.

"I'm not sure. Our schedules have been crazy since we've been back." Ashiree lifted a brow at her. So Chelsea explained further. "Jacen has been downtown a lot. Something to do with the second location he wants for the club, and I've extended my editing services to YA and fantasy." That news perked Ashiree's interest.

"Really? Any good storylines so far?"

"Yes." She answered, and they spend the rest of the night discussing some of the books she'd come across, excluding specifics about the author, title, or character names.

~~~~~~~~~~~~~~~~~~~~~~

Jacen shuddered as he trotted up the walkway to the community center and quickly entered the building. The chilling icy wind prepared everyone for the snow due to fall later that evening.

"You're late?"

"I do have a business to run, Shayna." He told his sister-in-law, who didn't seem at all concerned with his statement.

"We're using the art room as the setup for the wardrobe. Please hurry. We want to get at least three themes done today." She answered him by signing off on some form on a clipboard handed to her by a young lady.

"Alright. Is Chelsea here?"

"Yes. Unlike some people, she showed up on time. When you're dressed, come to the main gym. We have things set up there." Shayna responded. Jacen nodded and headed in the opposite direction of where Shayna was heading. When he reached the art room, it looked like a war zone. Clothes, costumes, and theme prompts were everywhere.

"Oh, you finally made it thank God." Jacen heard Asia say, practically dragging him into the room. She handed him the first outfit for the St. Patrick's Day theme when he saw Chelsea step from behind a scrim in the corner. Jacen could help but stop and stare. She was the sexiest dressed leprechaun he'd ever seen. His eyes slowly scanned her body up and down. Her sandy brown hair covered her shoulders and landed just above the top line of the green dress. Bringing very much attention to her cleavage. The black belt snatched her waist perfectly accentuated her hips covered in a wide ruffled skirt, and her legs looked amazing in white thigh stockings with a pair of sexy black pumps.

"I feel ridiculous." She admitted walking over to him. Somehow, he'd seen the whole image of her walking over to him in slow motion even though she was walking at an average pace.

"You look anything but." He told her, finally finding his voice. She smiled shyly.

"Mr. Turner." He heard his name called with a sense of urgency from Asia.

"I guess I better hurry up." He said, chuckling.

"Yes, You should. You know Shayna runs a tight schedule." He nodded at Chelsea's response with a chuckle. He turned back to head behind his own scrim with a bit of nudging from Asia. He did his best not to laugh. Shayna kept everyone on edge, and he couldn't blame her. She took pride in everything she did. Changing, he kept replaying his initial site of Chelsea in his mind. She thought she looked ridiculous. She was wrong; in fact, he was the one looking ridiculous in the outfit Shayna selected. There was no way in the world he was wearing this.

"I don't see what the problem is."

"Seriously, Shayna!" Chelsea listened as Shayna and Jacen went back and forth on her choice of Jacen's costume. In Chelsea's opinion, he looked hot. Black slacks with black shoes complemented by a clover decorated bowtie and suspenders. The bowtie she liked, but agreed the suspenders were an absolute no-go.

"I have an idea." Asia said, trying to help the situation. She brought over a black vest with clovers on it."

"We chose not to use this because the hat wasn't measured right. If we use the vest, we have to use the hat." Shayna explained as Chelsea watched Jacen remove the suspenders and put on the vest. Not even bothering to go behind the scrim. She did her best not to gawk. A bare-chested Jacen was hot, but a slightly vest-covered chest Jacen looked utterly sexy. The vest allowed for more focus on his arms, and to Chelsea, it was perfect.

"What if Chelsea wears the hat instead?" Asia suggested. The three of them turned to her. She smiled slightly, picked up the top-hat, placed it on her head, and slightly extended her arms.

"That might work." Shayna said, rubbing her chin. "Chelsea, come stand here." She further instructed. Chelsea did as suggested, coming to stand beside Jacen. She tried her best to keep the butterflies in her stomach from simmering.

"The hat with the heels helps with the height difference." Asia commented. Shayna nodded and agreed. As they continued to talk, Chelsea tried desperately to listen. Her nearness to Jacen was recking havoc on her sense and ability to focus. She was standing very close to him, and the scent of his aftershave caused her to inwardly groan. There was nothing better than a good-smelling man. Add to that a slightly bare-chested sexy one, the perfect package. Eventually, Shayna and Asia agreed, and they all headed to the gym, allowing Chelsea a few minutes to regain her sanity and attempt to get through the photoshoot.

Chapter Twelve

"Can you look this way, Mr. Turner?" Jacen did his best to focus as the cameraman took yet another picture of him. He angled his head as the director instructed, wondering where Chelsea went. After photos were taken of them for March and April, the May cover would only include him. He had to admit he preferred his current attire then the St. Patrick's Day outfit.

All in all, it turned out well, except for him constantly fighting with himself to focus on the cameraman instead of Chelsea. He blew out a breath as he turned again, posing in the suggested position. A few more clicks of the camera, and Shayna announced they were done. He sighed in relief.

"You did well. Not as enthusiastic as I hoped, but it worked better for the shot." Shayna said.

"I aim to please." He said jokingly while standing to exit the gym area. Shayna fell into step with him.

"We're expecting to shoot for October, November, and December months, with Halloween being next week. Don't forget!" Shayna insisted.

"Should I be worried about the wardrobe?" Jacen asked.

"No. Since I know who your date is, it's easier to plan for certain outfits. One of the reasons I don't like to wait until the last minute." Shayna responded as they approached the art room where Jacen would change.

"If Chelsea hadn't agreed, I wouldn't have a date." he says earnestly. Shayna paused just outside the door of the art room.

"Be careful with her, Jacen. Chelsea isn't like the other woman you've tangled with." Shayna warned again. Jacen looked at his sister-in-law and nodded. He pondered momentarily if the warning was general or if Shayna knew about Chelsea's family.

"I know she's not." He reassured. Shayna eyed him skeptically before nodded and giving him the location of the next photoshoot. He agreed and stepped into the Art room. Chelsea was partially laughing at something with Asia. Dressed in the clothes he assumed she'd arrived in, she looked comfortable and carefree. They both acknowledged his presence as he went behind his scrim to change.

When he finished, Asia wasn't around, and Chelsea was standing by the door.

"You survived." she teased.

"Barely." He responded with a light chuckle. He watched as she reached on the table behind her and grabbed a scarf. She also handed him his coat that he hadn't noticed was on the table.

"Are you heading over to the club?" Chelsea asked.

"Just long enough to make sure everything is set up for tomorrow night." Jacen answered.

"That's right, you have that big birthday bash for that football player." Chelsea said. Jacen smiled and nodded. Ever since his best friend and football player Trent Taylor held his celebration party at Ensconce last year, the demand for his club was high. It was why Jacen was looking for a second location. Something to exclusively cater to more celebrity parties and events. His current club was charming, held a nice ambiance, but everything was about presentation. He could only accommodate one VIP section and wanted to change that.

"Yes. What are you doing after this?" He asked.

"I'm not sure yet. Ashiree is studying for a test, so I might just be hanging solo."

"How about you have dinner with me tonight?" He suggested.

"Are you asking me out on a date?"

"I am. I've been a terrible boyfriend." Jacen said teasingly.

"No, you haven't." She assured him. "I would love to have dinner with you." Chelsea replied. They agreed on a time and left out of the community center to their cars.

~~~~~~~~~~~~~~~~~~~~~~~~

Chelsea accepted Jacen's help as she sat in the seat at the famous seafood restaurant. The photoshoot earlier that day was more exhausting than she had remembered. In her college years, she had been the girl helping behind the scenes, watching as Shayna or another executive gave instructions on how they wanted the picture to look. She never once considered how the models felt. It had taken three hours of posing, changing, angling, tilting your head, shifting, standing, crouching, only to have to switch costumes and do it all over again. Jacen took his seat across from her as the waiter handed them menus and asked for their drink order.

"Have you eaten here before?" Jacen asked as she was glancing over her menu. She shook her head and looked up.

"Do you have any recommendations?" She asked. He gave her a few suggestions as she looked back down over the menu, she agreed, and told the waiter when he returned.

"I've been meaning to ask you something." Jacen began.

"Okay. What is it?" Chelsea answered.

"What do you do for a living? It's something that crossed my mind earlier. Show Stoppin closed almost three years ago. And I know for a fact you are not on the diner or the club's payroll." Jacen said. Chelsea slightly chuckled.

"I'm a book editor." she answered nervously.

"Really?" He asked, surprised. "What kind of books?"

"Mainly romance, but I come across a good mystery every now and then. I've recently started taking on young adult and some fantasy novels."

"Wow. I don't think I've ever met a book editor before." He admitted.

"Well, it's not too different from a magazine editor." She answered. It was completely different, but she wanted to give him some connection to her former job and the current one.

"I never thought about that. Shayna was the top editor at Show Stoppin'. I guess I just never considered what she actually did for her job." Jacen admitted.

"It's a lot of work, but I learned a lot. Plus, I love to read." She admitted.

"What's your favorite thing to read?" He asked, genuinely interested.

"Romance." She admitted shyly.

"A hopeless romantic?" He asked.

"No, I am a hopeful romantic. I don't understand how I can be hopeless for something I actually want." She stated. It was one of her biggest pet peeves when people said hopeless romantic.

"I've never heard of that. But I like it." Jacen said with smile. His pearly whites brought butterflies to her stomach.

"Ashiree says I'm weird for it." Chelsea said quickly. Trying to calm down her nerves and not stare at Jacen. The man was too good-looking. It was hard enough controlling her attraction to him, but then, he smiled and she was goner.

"How?"

"It always rubs me the wrong way when I hear people say things that actually mean the opposite of what they are saying." She gave him a few examples.

"I didn't realize how much we all say things like that. I guess I have to be careful with certain sayings with you." He teased.

"You don't have to do that. It happens all the time. I guess it's just the editor in me. I get the same little cringe when I see the wrong grammar used in the books I edit."

"What do you mean?"

"Like, your and you're, to, too and two, and my absolute favorite, their, there or they're." Jacen laughed at her slightly annoyed expression.

"I would hate for you to see any of my old English papers from high school." She playful cringed and he laughed just as the waiter approached with their food.

~~~~~~~~~~~~~~~~~~~~~~~~~

They walked alongside the small pier right outside the restaurant. The cool nights' air was perfect for a late October night. They walked in silence, and they stopped and leaned against the dock. The crescent moon reflected in the water off the harbor. The water hitting the sides of the boats, and a few seagulls gawked in the back.

"How did you enjoy the photoshoot?" Jacen said.

"It was nice, I guess." She answered honestly.

"You guess?" He questioned.

"Yes, I mean, I know how crazy it can be in the background assisting with the props and helping setup. But being on the other side of the camera is a different experience altogether." Jacen chuckled at her words.

"I understand what you mean. I should have thought to ask Dany to help you out." Jacen stated. Chelsea gasped.

"I'm glad you didn't." Chelsea said honestly. Jacen looked over at her with a quirked brow.

"Why?"

"She's an ex-supermodel and an amazing one at that. I'd be too embarrassed about making a mistake."

"Isn't Onica the same?"

"Yes, but I'd never had to worry about performing in front of Onica." She admitted. She turned back to look out into the harbor. Old memories of fake fashion shows and wardrobe changes she's seen as a child replayed in her mind. It was a little pastime for her sisters to play dress-up with Onica clothes and shoes, sometimes a little makeup. Ronica always chose the clothes, and Sonica and Monica would fake strut in front of the massive mirror in Onica's bedroom closet. She was never invited to participate as Monica would remind her that Onica was not her mom and only her daughters could play in her clothes. Ronica and Sonica never disputed or argued against Monica, so she would flee from her hiding spot and go find Lorelai.

"Chelsea, Chelsea!" She blinked, realizing Jacen had been speaking to her. His brows deepened in concern.

"I'm sorry, what?" She asked, shaking herself from her thoughts.

"Where did you just go?" He asked in a very concerned voice.

"Nowhere. I was just lost in the sound of the water for a minute." She lied. She couldn't tell him about her thoughts. She honestly didn't want to think about them. His eyes stayed on her for a few more seconds before he decided to let the matter go and ask her again about the upcoming photoshoot. She was grateful to change the subject, but she could tell he knew she had been thinking more than what she'd admitted. Light snow began to fall around them, bringing an end to their evening. They were quiet as Jacen drove her home. He'd walked her to her doorstep, kissed her politely on her cheek, waited until she was safely inside and locked the door before heading back to his vehicle. She couldn't help but watch from the front window as he got into his truck and pulled away. Sighing, she headed up the stairs to her bedroom. She usually put in a couple of hours of editing, but tonight she didn't have it in her. She decided to run a bath, adding her favorite scented bath bombs, and even lit a few candles. Shedding her clothes and submerging herself in the warm water, she wondered if she should have been honest with Jacen. No one knew everything she'd endured as a child with Monica's antics, not even Ashiree. She closed her eyes, rested her head on the back of the tub, and let her worries melt away, if only for that night.

~~~~~~~~~~~~~~~~~~~~~~~~~~~

"So you decided to date Chelsea for the Calendar?" Trent said, coming to sit in the recliner after grabbing a beer in the new man cave of his home.

"Yes." Jacen admitted, taking a swig of his root beer.

"Just for the Calendar, or is there more?" Jacen chuckled, knowing from Trent's tone he already suspected the answer.

"There might be more." He answered honestly. His date with Chelsea the other night had been enjoyable. Finding out more things about her. Seeing her true passion behind her work. She was interesting, and he couldn't say that about a lot of the women he dated.

"I heard Shayna gave you a not-so-nice warning." Trent says with a slight tease.

"Twice." Jacen stated with two fingers. He almost asked how Trent knew so much when he'd barely been home all season, but then he quickly remembered Trent probably heard it from Kaitlyn, who heard it from her sister Kaycee, one of Shayna's best friends. He never really thought about how genuinely close-knit everyone was until that moment. Even Donovan was now married to Danyelle, Trent's little sister.

"She's pretty." Trent said absentmindedly, bringing Jacen out of his thoughts.

"I know. I don't understand how I've missed that. I've known Chelsea for years."

"Shocking isn't it. It's like a light bulb goes off." Trent said, taking another swig of his beer. Jacen nodded, knowing Trent felt that way the moment he'd noticed Kaitlyn. They'd all grown up together, and even though Kaitlyn had the biggest crush on Trent as kids and well into their teenage years, Trent never noticed or hadn't considered Kaitlyn. He pondered for a second if Chelsea harbored a crush on him. She was sweet and friendly, pleasant to be around, easy to talk to. But she was like that with everyone. No one ever had a bad thing to say about Chelsea. Even his bouncers mentioned that she was always making it a point to speak to them, even if just to say hello.

Thundering footsteps broke his thoughts as he and Trent shifted their gaze toward the stairs to see Mikey, Trey, and Jay Jay barging into the room. Mikey was Trent and Kaitlyn's six-year son. Trey was Justin and Alexia's son, and Jay Jay was James and Kaycee's son.

"Uncle Jaceeeennnn!" Mikey yelled and beat on his chest like Tarzan. Jacen stood as Mikey beelined straight toward him and launch himself at Jacen for a hug. Jacen caught him laughing. Mikey was all theatrics.

"Hey, buddy. How are you?" He said, hugging him tightly. Mikey gripped him tighter, and Jacen returned it until Mikey laughed and tapped out.

"One day, I'm gonna win at that." He announced. Jacen smiled and released him. Mikey ran, launching himself onto his dad's lap. He saw Trent quickly shift his beer to his other hand to settle

Mikey. Jacen then picked up Trey and got a slight hug while high-five-ing Jay Jay.

"What are you boys up to?" Jacen asked, putting Trey back on his feet.

"Mikey got us in trouble, so auntie Kay sent us down here." Jay Jay explained as he and Trey sat down in front of them.

"Michael!" Jacen heard Trent's firm voice as he spoke to his son. "What did you do?"

"I didn't mean to break it." He began to explain to his father. Trent placed his beer down and plopped Mikey on the floor with a stern look.

"I'll be right back." Trent said, crossing the room and heading up the stairs. Jacen looked at each boy and saw the devastation in their eyes. Whatever they broke, it wasn't good. He remembered the same look on his face when he, Trent, and Donovan had gotten in trouble for shooting water guns in the Taylor Estate. They'd ruin some silk drapes that Constance Taylor had custom-made for her parlor room. Footsteps had them all turning their heads as Trent stood halfway down the stairs and called for Mikey. The little boy got up, walking slowly to his father. All the exuberant and ecstatic energy gone from him. He followed his father back up the stairs quietly as if he were walking the plank to his death. Once out of sight and up the stairs, Jacen looked at Jay Jay.

"What did he break?"

"One of great-grandma glass elephants." Jay Jay answered worryingly. Jacen's eyes widened, knowing Mikey definitely was walking the plank.

"Yeah, auntie Kay was crying." Trey said solemnly, and Jacen nodded. It was one thing to break something that Kaitlyn held dear, but a totally different issue if she cried. That would upset Trent more than anything else. Friends, family, or even his son, nobody made Kaitlyn cry.

Chapter Thirteen

"One more shot and you're toast." Chelsea smiled as she watched Ashiree and her date play pool. It was a slow wednesday evening at Victor's Billiards and Pool Hall.

"Ha, you wish!" Ashiree said. Caden was a new guy in Ashiree's apartment building who had spent the last few weeks trying to get Ashiree to go out with him. He was tall, nicely built, and looked pretty good, slightly bent over a pool table. He was constantly sending flirtatious looks in Ashiree's direction. Chelsea almost felt sorry for the guy; Ashiree was not interested. Hence why she was there, basically the planted third wheel.

"Crap." Chelsea heard Caden say in annoyance, he'd just missed his shot at the eight ball.

"Watch and learn, rookie." Ashiree said, slowly and meticulously aiming her cue at the eight ball. Just to make Caden sweat a little bit more, Ashiree glanced his way, looking dead in his eyes as she took her shot, knocking the eight ball in the corner pocket. Chelsea did her best not to laugh at poor Caden's expression.

"Man, you're good." Caden admitted with slight flirtation in his voice. Chelsea shook her head; he was a goner.

"Or maybe she just needs a heftier dose of competition." Chelsea's head whipped around to see Jacen and his friend Donovan Fields walking over to their area.

"Are you challenging me, Donovan?" Ashiree asked. Donovan answered yes, introductions were made, and Chelsea watched Ashiree, Donovan, Caden, and Jacen play three rounds. In the last round, Donovan and Ashiree went neck and neck.

"There is no way you're going to make that shot, Ashiree." Donovan said with a cocky smile. Ashiree was standing with her pool cue upright, biting her lip, slight frustration edging on her face. Chelsea looked at the pool table. The shot seemed impossible, but hit at the right angle, she could pull it off.

"It's not impossible." Chelsea stated, rendering four sets of eyes to glance her way.

"Since when did you start playing pool?" Jacen asked.

"I don't. It's just angles." Chelsea responded.

"I'm willing to bet you can't make that shot." Donovan challenged.

"I'm willing to bet she can." Ashiree countered.

"I don't play pool. It was just an observation."

"Come on, Chelsea, you've been sitting over here watching all night. If you see the shot, take it." Jacen encouraged. "Plus, Don can't make that either."

"Dude, who's side are you on?" Donovan said.

"You can't make that shot, and you want Ashiree to blow it so you can get it from another angle.

"That's exactly the point." Donovan concurred.

"Thank you for the vote of confidence, Jacen." Ashiree said. Jacen just shrugged his shoulders and turned back to Chelsea.

"So what's it going to be, huh, Chels?" Jacen challenged.

"Fine." Chelsea sighed. Pool wasn't her game; no game was actually her game. Sliding off the stool she'd been perfectly happy sitting on, she walked over to take Ashiree cue.

"You're going to need a shorter stick." Jacen and Ashiree both said. She almost glared at them. It was one of the reasons she chose to sit out. She was forever the short one at 5'3'. Jacen stood the tallest at 6' 4'. Donovan wasn't far behind at around 6'2', and Caden stood almost as tall as Donovan. Even standing next to Ashiree at her 5' 8' height made Chelsea feel like a midget. Grabbling a cue from the cue stand, she chalked it to her liking and walked over to the pool table. Looking again at her angles, she decided to use the angle from where she'd sat. Asking politely for Jacen to move over, she took a breath, slowly bent over, and lined her cue stick up. No one spoke, understanding the importance of concentration at this moment. Focusing on her shot, she inhaled slightly, then exhaled while taking her shot. The white ball hit four different sides of the pool table before finally knocking the eight ball in the corner pocket.

"Yes!!" Ashiree practically shouted, coming around the table to hug her.

"I can't believe she made that shot." Donovan said, completely stunned.

"Neither can I." Caden added.

"This right here is my secret weapon." Ashiree boasted proudly.

"Nice job, Chelsea." Jacen congratulated.

"You've been holding out on us, Chelsea." Donovan said.

"Honestly, I'm not that good." Chelsea admitted.

"I think that shot says otherwise." Caden said.

"She is always great at the impossible shots, but give her a straight shot, she blows it every time." Ashiree said teasingly.

"This is true." Chelsea agreed.

"Well, I think we'll call it a night." Ashiree said. Caden seemed pleased, and Chelsea felt sorry for him again. He was going home alone whether he knew it or not.

"I probably should also. Dany's had enough of a break from me." At Donovan's statement, a few brows lifted. "She likes to kick me out of the house for a couple hours a week. I'm totally fine being at home with my girls, though." Donovan further explained. Dany, or better yet, ex-supermodel Danyelle Taylor, settled pretty well as a wife and mother of two after leaving her model career during her prime, as some would say.

"What about you, Chelsea? Are you calling it a night?" Jacen asked.

"I guess so. I mean, everyone else is."

"Stay and play a game with me."

"I'm really not that good." She admitted.

"You know what they say, practice makes perfect." he said.

"Okay." She agreed, shrugging her shoulders. She hugged Ashiree and Donovan goodbye and said her farewells to Caden as Jacen racked the balls for their game.

~~~~~~~~~~~~~~~~~~~~~~~~

Jacen ordered another drink for Chelsea as he watched her take another lousy shot. Ashiree was right. The simplest shots she missed.

"I still don't understand how you missed that shot." Jacen teased. Chelsea shrugged.

"It's a curse." She said nonchalantly. He picked up his stick and cued another ball into the slot.

"Have you ever tried not going for the simple shot?" He asked and saw her lift a brow.

"What do you mean?" she asked.

"Take a look at this ball." He pointed. It was the closet striped ball to any slot on the table. "What's the obvious slot?" he asked. Chelsea pointed to the slot on the right side in the middle.

"So, when you take your shot, that's the one you would pick?" he asked.

"Yes, it's the closest." She answered, shrugging her shoulders, not following his train of thought.

"But where else could you pocket it?" he asked, watching as her face slightly contorted in thought. He could see her mind working and knew she was concentrating really hard.

"This one." She pointed to a pocket on the left closet to her. Jacen furrowed his brows for just a second, not seeing how she would make the shot but believing she could.

"Go for it." Jacen encouraged. He watched her nervously switch sides to line up the shot she wanted. Nerves shifted into pure concentration as she focused and then took her shot. The ball hit four different sides before finally sinking in the left corner pocket.

"Oh, my gosh, I did it."

"Yes, you did and very well." He praised.

"Wow, I never thought to do that." She admitted. He nodded.

"Most people try and go for the easier shots."

"Which I suck at." She said.

"True, but you see the angles different than most, and you have to work what's best for you." She beamed at him, and he could see her confidence proudly displaying on her face.

"Let's play again." She said.

"Technically, this game isn't over. It's your turn again." He answered.

"Right." She countered, now taking a different look over the balls left on the pool table. She had four striped left to his two. With her new perspective on playing the game, Jacen took a step back and just watched as, one by one, she pocketed the remaining four of her balls and then the eight ball. Leaving his two solid balls lonely and untouched.

~~~~~~~~~~~~~~~~~~~~~~~~~~~~~

"I told you. You are better than you thought you were." Jacen said as they were heading to her brownstone. Jacen offered to give her a ride after they decided to leave the pool hall.

"I think you helped me unlock my secret mojo." she answered.

"Glad I can help. Maybe it will reduce the balance on my leger." He said teasingly.

"What leger?" she asked as he pulled up and parked in front of her home.

"Chelsea, you have been helping me out at the diner and the club since Trent's wedding. Without any form of payment. I'm almost ashamed to admit I hadn't even realized it until recently."

"I told you I don't mind, I still don't. Plus, you needed the help."

"But you continued, why?" he asked, pure confusion on his face. She shrugged, not fully knowing how to answer him. She honestly hadn't mind helping. For the most part, it helped in getting her out of her brownstone. Other than her outings with Ashiree, she didn't have much of a social life like. But she knew none of that mattered. She could visit a park, possibly do some volunteering, anything other than hanging around his diner. She liked seeing Jacen though. It was the perfect excuse to be around him, hear his voice, and watch him work. He was such a smart man, and he was kind, proving the best working environment he could. Several of his employees in both the diner and the club mentioned more than once how great of a boss Jacen was, compared to their previous employers and work experience. She could wholeheartedly agree with them, and that made her want to be around him even more. She hadn't planned on staying; it just sort of happened. It became a routine for her.

The silence in the car grew between then, and she wondered for a second if he no longer wanted her help. Technically he was fully staffed, and most of the time, she just helped pick up a little bit of slack, but she wasn't needed anymore.

"Do you want me to stop?" she asked, looking down in her lap as her hands slightly gripped her purse. She couldn't look at him, knowing that even though they were pretending to date during the calendar events, it didn't mean he really wanted her around.

"No, Chelsea. I was just curious. I like when you're there. I've actually grown accustomed to it. It seems at times you know more about what going on than I do." He admitted.

"I can't explain it. I like it too." She said, looking over at him, feeling slightly less nervous about him actually wanted her around.

"I just can't figure how to repay you since I know you won't let me put you on staff." She laughed at his teasing. He'd suggested a few times about paying her a salary.

"Trust me, the weekend with my family was payment enough. I'm sure you saw more drama in two days with me than you've seen in the last two months at the club." She stated. Jacen huffed out a small laugh in agreement.

"Okay, you win." He conceited.

"I did win tonight, three-times to be exact." She said, holding up three fingers. After finding what she now saw as her secret mojo, she played three more games with Jacen and won all of them.

"Are you boasting over there, Chelsea Stone?"

"A little." She said proudly. He didn't say anything. He just shook his head and smiled.

"Do you want to come in?" she asked. The question popped out of her mouth before she had a chance to catch herself. She watched the slight shock on Jacen's face at her words turn into an expression she couldn't read.

"We can discuss the next photoshoot." She quickly added.

"Sure, Chelsea. I'd love to come in." Jacen answered.

Chapter Fourteen

Jacen Turner crossed the threshold of Chelsea's brownstone, mildly shocked by her invitation. He'd actually been thinking of a way to get her to ask him to come in. He hadn't wanted the night to end, and he wanted to talk to her about something. The thought of discussing the upcoming photoshoot hadn't crossed his mind, but it was a good idea for them to discuss it. Taking a look around, the brownstone held three levels. The foyer displayed a staircase to the right, heading to the other floors, and an open floorplan with a kitchen, a small dining area, and a living room on the left. Chelsea explained the second level held three bedrooms, while the third floor housed another living space and a small Galleria of arts and paintings that her aunt collected over the years.

Chelsea offered Jacen a drink, and they began to discuss the upcoming photoshoot and what to expect at the children's hospital for the cookie drive. Jacen was intrigued by Chelsea's interests and also learned she volunteered at a children's shelter and the local retirement home.

"I have a question to ask, Chelsea?" he began, as Chelsea grabbed another can of pop for him and refilled her wine glass.

"Do you?" she answered, handing him the can and heading toward the couch. She folded her legs under her as she got comfortable.

"Yes, I feel as your boyfriend, I should know." He said with a tease.

"Pulling the boyfriend card on me again?" she asked.

"Yeah, but if you chose not to answer, I can respect it." He watched as the seriousness in his tone shifted the expression on her face.

"Okay, what do you want to ask me?" she said, leaning back against the couch.

"What happened between you, Monica and Casey?" if he expected some sort of shock or surprise on her face at his question, he didn't get it. She looked down at the glass in her hand for a while before looking back up at him and telling him what he wanted to know.

Chelsea began to explain the dynamic of the relationship, first starting with Monica. Jacen learned that Monica basically tormented Chelsea her entire childhood. Little planks were played against her, like putting bubble gum in her hair, bugs in her bed, and ruining some of her school projects. These incidents were ignored and allowed because her father traveled and the only person to do anything was Onica. Chelsea explained that she never fully understood why her sister hated her so much. Even today, she wasn't sure what prompted Monica to have a personal vendetta against her.

The situation with Casey happened around the time when she was eighteen years old. She missed her father and begged her aunt to send her to him for the summer. She met Casey and his brothers when they all went to a local beach party. Casey instantly liked Chelsea, and being the shy girl, she really enjoyed his attention. She thought he loved her, thought she loved him. He had been her first, and she foolishly believed they would be together. Chelsea had not been aware of Monica's interest in Casey. By the end of the summer, she'd lost her first boyfriend, her virginity, and her heart. She hadn't come back to her father's home again until Ronica's wedding.

"I'm so sorry, Chelsea." Jacen admitted after she'd finished telling him. He could have guessed that

Casey had been her first, but he never thought she would have caught him kissing her sister.

"It was almost ten years ago, Jacen."

"That doesn't mean it still doesn't hurt." He said, she shook her head.

"I'm over Casey, it was puppy love, and that's never meant to last."

"Says the hopeful romantic." He teased. She smiled at him and the light in her eyes return. She seemed so tormented as she recalled the beginning drama of her family with him. He still didn't like that Monica was allowed to treat her with so much disrespect. With three older brothers, he couldn't imagine them doing anything out of hatred or evil intent toward him. Sure they teased him, that's what brothers did, but they'd also be the first ones to protect him.

"You've got me there." She started and finished the last contents of her glass. He noticed the time on his watch and decided he should go. Though Chelsea smiled, he could still see the recap took a toll on her emotions. That hadn't been his intent, he was just curious, but he honestly should have known it would be worse than he assumed.

"I should go." He said, standing slowly. She nodded and did the same. She took the can from him as they passed the kitchen on the way to her front door.

"Thank you for the ride home." She said.

"Anytime." He said. He turned as she stood beside him at her front door. He didn't like the wariness in her eyes. He knew he'd caused it. Taking his arm, he gently tugged her toward him, and she went willingly in his arms. He liked this feeling. Like the growing attraction, he had for her.

"I want to kiss you, Chelsea." He admitted. He saw her eyes avert to his lips for just a second before returning to his eyes. She nodded and he leaned down to kiss her lips softly. Loving the smooth feeling of them pressed against his. Her soft whimper made him pull her closer to him. Bringing their bodies as close as they could get with clothes on. Jacen felt Chelsea's arms go around his neck, her hand cradling his head as if to mold her mouth to his, opening her mouth to allow his tongue to mingle with hers, he obliged, kissing her urgently and wantonly. A chime in the background blared, causing Chelsea to end their kiss and released him. Jacen groaned in protest, still holding her to him, and rested his forehead against hers.

"I'm sorry. That's probably Ashiree checking on me. I haven't texted her that I made it home yet."

"I understand." He said, lifting his head, slightly loosening his grip on her. Her arms that were wrapped around his neck now rested on his arms.

"I'll see you tomorrow." She said.

"Yes, you will." He agreed, leaning down to kiss her again. "I could get used to this." He added. She smiled and stepped back, forcing him to release her. Her phone blared again, and they both laughed.

"I better get that, another missed call, and she'll be driving over here." She said with a chuckle.

"She's a good friend." Jacen stated, straightening his jacket.

"The best friend." Chelsea confirmed.

"Lock up behind me." He said, opening her door to leave.

"I will. Goodnight, Jacen." She said.

"Goodnight Chelsea."

~~~~~~~~~~~~~~~~~~~~~~~

Chelsea took a seat on the bench in the park Jacen found for them. The cookie drive had been a success. Helping the kids at the children's hospital was something she loved and remembered the first time she'd ever come when she worked with Shayna right after college. The kids loved Jacen. He was fun and playful with them. Never letting their current diagnosis stop him from fully embracing the moment with them.

"I think this is one of the best cookies I've ever had." Jacen said with a mouth half full of cookies. Chelsea took a bite of her own and groaned inwardly at the softness of the cookie.

"It's pretty good, I have to agree."

"Do you bake? I think I recall your aunt used to." Chelsea smiled at Jacen's mention of her aunt.

"Yes, my aunt used to bake, and she was very good at it, but her skills and love for baking did not pass on to me."

"Really? Who did they pass to?"

"Ashiree." She declared happily.

"Wow, I didn't know Ashiree could bake."

"Yup." she concurred, nodding her head and taking a bite of another cookie.

"How long have you two been friends?" Jacen asked, popping his last cookie in his mouth. Chelsea blinked twice, realizing how fast he ate them.

"Since we were thirteen years old." Chelsea answered.

"That's a long time. Almost as long as Trent and me." Jacen responded.

"Yes, it is. We always tell people we bonded over flour, sugar, and chocolate." She laughed as she said it.

"I'm sure that makes for a great introduction." Jacen teased.

"She's the bravest person I know." Chelsea admitted.

"I'm not sure about that, Chelsea. You're pretty brave yourself." Jacen stated.

"Maybe, but not like Ashiree."

"I heard she had it a little rough growing up." Jacen said.

"She did. I don't think the foster system is ever easy to grow up in. I had my family issues, but I had my aunt to fall back on. Ashiree lived in twelve different homes growing up."

"Whoa. That's a lot. I can't even imagine." Jacen admitted.

"Neither can I. I remember the day Ashiree found out she was leaving the Carters' home. They were the foster couple that lived next door to my aunt and me. I was devastated."

"How long had she lived there?"

"Almost two years." Chelsea stated.

"I'm guessing that was hard." Jacen says.

"For me? Yes. For Ashiree, not so much. I guess, in a way, she was used to it. But I wasn't. I told her I would write to her since I wasn't sure if she'd be able to use the phone where she was going next. She nodded at me, and I could tell she didn't believe me. After balling my eyes out for hours after she left, I told my aunt how I felt. She says Ashiree probably had several friends growing up, each promising to keep in touch but didn't. I was determined to not be that friend. I wasn't the best person to walk up and meet someone new or strike up a conversation with a stranger, but I knew I could write a letter, and I decided, no matter what, I was going to keep in touch."

"It must have worked. You two are still friends."

"Yes, we are. She's my best friend, closer to me like a sister, more so than my own." Chelsea felt Jacen's hand clasp over hers. She stared off into the park as memories of her childhood, both good and bad, flooded her mind. Ashiree had been her happy point. The one person, no matter what, loved her. Sure her aunt did, and she was sure her father did, but outside of them, Ashiree was it.

"I'm glad you have her in your life." Jacen said, interrupting her thoughts. She looked at him. Her eyes met his, and a sly smile appeared on his face. He really was a handsome man. She couldn't think of a more romantic moment. It reminded her of the scenes in the novel she was editing. If this scene were a replica, he would lean over slowly, hear her sharp intake of breath just before his lips connected with hers. She blinked, realizing Jacen asked her a question.

"I'm sorry, what did you say?" She asked, slightly flushed and embarrassed.

"I asked if you were ready to get out of here?"

"Oh sure, of course." She said, removing her hand from his and quickly standing.

"What do you have going on tonight?"

"Nothing much, just some editing." She saw him nodding at her response as he also stood.

"Well..." he began. He seemed a little nervous. "...If you don't have any plans, would you like to join me for dinner with my parents?" She blinked again. Surprised he would ask her. Sure they were dating, and she'd been to Tuesday night at his parents' home before, but he had never invited her personally. Was that a good idea? What if his mother had the wrong impression when the six weeks were up?

"Do you think that's a good idea?" She asked nervously.

"I don't see why it wouldn't be. It's not like you've never attended before."

"True, but never as your girlfriend."

"Are you scared my mother might have our wedding planned out?" He teased.

"Aren't you? I mean, I don't mind coming, but you know what people will say." She answered. He took a step closer to her. Close enough for the alluring scent of his cologne to wrap around her nostrils, causing certain parts of her body to ignite.

"I'm sure my mother had some ideas for all of us at one point. But what are you worried about people saying?"

"That I'm trying to become the next Turner wife." She answered in slight annoyance. One, because his closeness was wreaking havoc on her senses and two, because she didn't want people to think she had a grand plan to trap him. She knew once the calendar events were over, so we're they. She wasn't the woman for him. Sure she liked him, was fiercely attracted to him, and enjoyed his kisses. But who wouldn't? Most of the women in Boston wanted one Turner brother or another. And Jacen was the last one. They were only pretending. She knew Jacen didn't see any future with her, and she wasn't going to let a few kisses make her believe it might lead to something else.

"We both know that is not the case, Chelsea. There are always rumors and gossip about my brothers and me. I choose to ignore them." She nodded, deciding she needed to do the same. It wasn't going to happen anyway.

"So, dinner at my parents?" He asked, taking a slight step back. She smiled.

"Yes, I'll join you for dinner with your parents."

Chapter Fifteen

Jacen glanced over, watching Chelsea bob her head to the radio as they drove to his parent's house. He slowly exhaled as he turned onto the street. Her words weighed heavier on him than he wanted to admit. *That I'm trying to become the next Turner wife.* It should have made him leap with joy that she didn't expect something after the six weeks were up. They could be friends with no drama or chaos. But that's not what he felt. Not even close. For the first time, he actually pictured himself married. And not a mundane dream but an actual vision. He always knew he'd want the love he saw with his parents, as well as his brothers, for himself. He saw everything he always wanted depleting in just those few words because she didn't want it. Call him a little vain, but there weren't many, if any, women that he dated that didn't seem to want to sink their claws into him and never let go. It's why he'd always been upfront, never wanted to mislead women into thinking their time together was more or heading in a direction he knew it wouldn't go. His and Chelsea's relationship was similar. A favor for a favor, although he was sure he came up short compared to how she's helped him the last four months. The relationship should have been a simple arrangement. Just six weeks to get through the calendar events, do his civic duty for charity, keep Shayna off his back, and all worked out well. Everything would go back to the way it was. He sighed a little as he parked across from his parents' house. Did he really want that? He knew the answer before he fully formed the question. No, he didn't. He didn't want to go back to not knowing Chelsea. He didn't want to go back to not spending time with her. He didn't want to go back to where Chelsea wasn't his. And that was the issue. She wasn't his.

He watched as she unbuckled her seatbelt and glanced over at him. Her sandy brown curls fell slightly over her shoulder. The sun hitting her face at just the right angle, making Jacen swallow hard at how beautiful she was.

"Jacen, are you alright?"

"Yes." He answered and confirmed his lie with a nod. He was far from alright and didn't know what to do about it. He shook himself out of his trance, exited the car, and opened her door, assisting Chelsea out of his truck. He took her hand, ignoring the slightly confused look on her face, crossed the street, and walked up to his parents' home.

Entering without knocking, he greeted his family. His father and his brothers, first while announcing Chelsea. Not that he needed to, they knew who she was. Then he headed over to the kitchen with her and kissed his mother in greeting on the cheek. Shayna, Alexia, and Kaycee were also there, and he greeted them before his mother kicked him out of her kitchen but asked Chelsea to stay. He reconvened with his father and brothers in the living room. Watching highlights of the previous night's football game.

"I see you brought Chelsea with you." Jerome stated.

"Why does that surprise you? She's been here for dinner before." Jacen replied.

"True, but never as your date." James said.

"Well, you know we're dating for the calendar." Jacen answered with a mild shrug, downplaying the new feelings he was developing.

"Just the calendar?" Justin asked. He nodded, not wanting it to say more.

"Are you going to make it to the fireman's bar-be-que next Saturday?" his father asked.

"Yes, I plan to stop by." Jacen answered his father.

"Are you bringing Chelsea with you?" one of his brothers asked.

"I hadn't thought about it. But I probably will. Mom mentioned it when I saw her in the kitchen. She was joking about giving Chelsea her potato salad recipe just as she was kicking me out." Jacen half-laughed. All his brothers got quiet, and his father displayed a slight smile.

"What?" Jacen questioned, noticing they all stared at him.

"You do know what that means, right?" James asked.

"No, what does it mean?" he asked.

"Mom is about to start planning your wedding, that's what." Jerome stated. Jacen almost laughed; he'd joked with Chelsea earlier, saying the exact same thing.

"I don't mind." he said before he had a chance to catch himself. He looked over at her brothers; none of their expressions were joking or smiling.

"Dad, can we use your study for a minute?" Justin asked their father. He nodded, and Jacen and his brothers left the living room to head into his father's study. Justin was first to enter the room, Jerome next, Jacen after Jerome and James behind him. As James shut the door, Jerome walked over to the minibar. He poured himself a drink and then three others.

"Drink this." Jerome said, handing Jacen a drink as well as the others.

"He doesn't need a drink right now." James said as Jerome handed him a glass.

"We all need a drink right now." Jerome stated, passing the last glass to Justin. He raised his glass in salute and drank it in one gulp. The others did the same.

"Now," Jerome stated, taking a seat on the sofa and looking over at Jacen. "Do you have any idea what you've gotten yourself into?"

~~~~~~~~~~~~~~~~~~~~~~~~~~

Chelsea glanced around the store as Jacen asked questions to the clerk. They were at a local wine tasting, and Chelsea didn't realize how much Jacen knew about wine. She had definitely learned a lot. She also discovered that she preferred her wine with a slight bit of tart taste rather than sweet. Jacen seemed intrigued no matter what type of wine it was. There were several tables aligned against the wall in the venue with vendors of various different wines on display for tasting. Some proudly discussed the newest wine or their signature wine, complementing it with light snacks or cheese platters. She didn't know how many different wines there were, but she took a break as she felt a slight buzz hit her. She walked around, eyeing the multiple bottles, their wrappings, and their age. So much work went into making the wine. An old episode of 'I love Lucy' popped in her mind, the one with Lucy crushing the grapes with her feet and Lucy's face as she began crushing and feeling the grapes in between her toes. She wasn't the only person in the venue that thought of it. As one vendor explained the process of pressuring the wine, a lady asked if some wineries still had people crushing grapes with their feet. A few others besides Chelsea laughed, but the vendors did not confirm what other wineries did, just that their particular wine process did not include anyone physically crushing grapes with toes.

"Hey! Are you ready to go?" She turned to see Jacen standing beside her with a big bag.

"Yes." She answered, and he escorted her out of his truck while waving to a few people he knew. Opening her door, she hopped in his vehicle as he opened the back door and placed the bottles of wine on the floor behind her. Once she was settled, he closed both doors and jogged around to get into the driver's side.

"Hey, I have an idea!" He said as he placed his seat belt on and started the truck.

"What is it?" she asked. He paused for a second before answering.

"I want to show you something. Do you mind taking a slight detour before I take you home?"

"Sure. where are we going?"

"It's a surprise." he said, his smile bright reaching almost to his ears.

"Ok." she agreed, wondering what had him grinning so hard. He connected his phone through Bluetooth and played some hip-hop songs on the way to their destination. Chelsea bobbed her head and tapped her foot to the beat. She loved hip-hop, the real hip-hop music like Mos Def, Common, the

Fugees, and Outkast. It was such a difference when riding in the car with Ashiree. Ashiree loved RnB, mixed with oldies but goodies. Chelsea didn't knock her friend; they just had different tastes in music. When 'Killin Me Softly' played, the Lauryn Hill version, Chelsea sang aloud, not caring that she was utterly butchering the song. Jacen laughed and sang just as terribly and loudly as she did. Shortly after singing three more songs, totally off-key, Jacen pulled into a parking lot and cut the engine. Chelsea's eyebrows furrowed as she took in the building.

"Come on." Jacen said, eagerly exiting his car. She took her seat belt off as he made his way around to her side and opened her door. Taking his hand, he helped out of the truck. Together they walked over to stand in front of the building.

"What do you think?" he asked, seeming to jump out of his skin with excitement. She looked at the two-story structure, it wasn't run down, but it could definitely use a paint job. It was once a convenience store. It took her a minute to realize what Jacen was showing her.

"It's the club." she almost shouted, realizing that Jacen was sharing his dream with her.

"Yes." he said, drawing out a long breath and looking at the building. For a moment, she just stood looking at him as he seemed to be lost in his thoughts. The peace and hopeful look on his face warmed her heart. This was his dreaming coming to life.

"Do you have the keys yet?" She asked. He shook his head.

"Not yet. There is still some more red tape as the city calls it, but it won't be much longer."

"I'm happy for you." she said, squeezing his hand in support. He looked down at her with his big brown eyes.

"Thanks, Chelsea, I haven't shown anyone else." he admitted. She tried to hide the smile that formed on her face. She felt honored that he chose to share this with her. The next hour they walked around the building as Jacen talked. She didn't see everything that he saw, the color of the lights or other decor he planned to create with the new location. But she nodded and supported his dream. He took her home shortly after and asked if she was coming to diner later. She told him she couldn't as she had a few editing projects to work on. Now that she had expanded her services, she had double the projects she'd had before. Who knew the fantasy world of novels was so much more popular than that of romance or even YA? He nodded and kissed her cheek after arriving at her house. He told her he would call her tomorrow as the club would be open tonight. She watched as he pulled off and wondered for a second if he ever slept.

Chapter Sixteen

The weather was perfect for a winter wonderland photoshoot in Boston Common. The idea was to catch a few shots of Jacen walking by a few kids playing in the snow. Of course, with Chelsea with him, the shoot was more of a couples outing while kids in the background played in the snow. After about an hour and a few cups of hot chocolate, Jacen was getting frustrated.

"I'm just not catching the shot I want." Shayna explained. The park was blanketed with snow and the sun shining at a perfect angle. Jacen didn't know what Shayna wanted to capture in the shot, but the crew members and Asia were slightly frantic with idea suggestions. Jacen looked down at Chelsea, sipping her cup of hot chocolate. Her eyes were focused on the kids playing in the snow.

"You look like you want to join them." Jacen teased. Chelsea looked up at him with a smile.

"It wouldn't be too bad. It beats standing here freezing trying to figure out where Shayna wants us standing or posing next." she said.

"I think you're right." He responded and gently took her cup from her hand and handed it to one of the crew staff. "Come on." he said, taking her hand and bolting from the photo area.

"Oh my gosh, Jacen, what are you doing?" Chelsea exclaimed while trying to keep up with him.

"Rescuing the both of us." he said. He could hear Shayna yelling for them as they ran further in an opening of the park where children were playing. Chelsea slipped, trying to keep up with Jacen's long strides, and in attempting to prevent Chelsea from falling, Jacen lost his footing and fell with her.

"Chelsea, are you okay?" Jacen said as they both sat up in the snow.

"You made me fall."

"I was trying to catch you, sorry." he explained while attempting to stand. Chelsea laughed.

"Well, since we're already covered in snow." Jacen looked over at Chelsea's words just as she launched a snowball at him, hitting him right in the chin.

"Oh, you're gonna get it." Jacen exclaimed. Chelsea squealed and began to crawl away, trying to catch her footing to stand. Just as she stood, Jacen launched a snowball at her, hitting her right in the butt. He saw her whirl around in surprise, but she started this war, and he was going to finish it. Chelsea began gathering snow, and he did the same, but he was a little faster than her, and just as he was about to throw another ball at her, he felt the cold sting and moisture of another snowball. Caught off guard, he turned to the left to see a little girl with one hand on her hips and a snowball in her other hand.

"It's not nice to hit girls on the butt." she declared while throwing another snowball at him. He deflected her snowball but missed the one Chelsea launched at him. Wiping his face, he noticed Chelsea laughing while the other kids ran over toward them.

"Tiana, did you throw a snowball at that man?" One of the boys said.

"He hit her on the butt." she explained to the boy who was quite taller than her.

"That's probably his girlfriend." the boy said.

"So, it's against the rules." she yelled back at him.

"They might not play by our rules." he hollered back. "Now apologize, or I'm telling mom."

~ 203 ~

the boy said. The other children around looked nervous, but little Tiana did not seem to want to back down until the boy, who Jacen assumed was her brother, mentioned their mom. He inwardly smiled. Understanding exactly how she felt as a younger sibling when your older sibling pulled the mom card. She folded her arms and turned toward Jacen.

"Sorry." she mumbled. Jacen tried his best not to laugh and walked over to her and kneeled.

"Apology accepted, but you're right I didn't play by the rules." Jacen admitted. His admittance seemed to soften the little girl's stance. Chelsea walked over, and Jacen stood as she introduced herself to the kids and they did the same. They played around in the snow for a while, before it was time for the kids to head home. Jacen and Chelsea watched as they left the park.

"I might have to tell Ashiree I have a new best friend." Chelsea said.

"Oh, you like seeing me attacked by a little girl with a snowball."

"I feel she was justified."

"Oh, do you now?" Jacen said, grabbing her by her waist and pulling her close to him.

"You broke the rules." Chelsea stated. Jacen looked down at her. Loving the playful side of her. But the war wasn't over.

"I believe you broke the rules also, Chelsea." her eyes widened just as she felt a cold sting of the snowball he had hidden slid down the back of her sweater. She squealed, pushing Jacen away, and he bent over with laughter as she danced frantically in the snow to get the snowball out.

"This means war Jacen Turner." she expelled and began to reach down to grab some snow.

"Oh no, you don't." Jacen declared and launched himself at her knocking them both into the snow. Squirming, and trying to get away from him, he caught the hand she managed to gather some snow in and held it above her head while hovering over her.

"No fair. You're much bigger than me." Chelsea proclaimed as she tried to wiggle from his grip. Jacen laughed at her attempt to free herself and was allured entirely when she stopped, and her eyes connected with his. He heard her sharp intake of breath as their close proximity became very evident. The chilly air around them didn't matter. The sounds of the city didn't matter. Others around them didn't matter. The only thing that mattered to Jacen was having her like this. Locked in his arms, slightly shuttering at his touch and ready for the kiss he badly wanted to give her. He watched as her eyes studied his face, slightly avert to his lips, and in response, she slowly licked her own. Jacen almost groaned at the invitation and slowly descended his head, ready to taste the sweetness from her lips.

"Are you two kids done horsing around?" Shayna's words interrupted the pleasurable moment he was sure he would have enjoyed. Chelsea shifted beneath him, a bit uncomfortable with Shayna practically standing over them, and Jacen moved from above her.

"Your timing is impeccable Shayna." Jacen gripped, standing and helping Chelsea to stand also.

"Well, I didn't want you two to catch a cold. The banquet is in two weeks, and I need you both there...and healthy." Shayna said, then turned around to walk away. Jacen realized the photo crew was packing up, and most of the background set was taken down.

"Are we done for the day?" Jacen called after her. She turned around with a sly smile.

"Yes, I have all the shots I need." Jacen narrowed his eyes at her as she continued walking away. If his brother didn't love her so much, Jacen might consider strangling her.

~~~~~~~~~~~~~~~~~~~~~~~~~~

Chelsea almost tripped as she exited her car in the back of the club. Josh had called her and practically begged her to come in. They were at max capacity and could really use the help. She eagerly agreed after the phone call she'd received early. Sonica had returned from her honeymoon with Nigel to find out Casey had left Monica and was serving her divorce papers. Shocked and rendered speechless, it took Chelsea a minute to take in the surprise that Sonica had even reached out to her. They talked for over an hour, which was the first time that had ever happened. Sonica sounded worried about her mom and their dad and how everything was falling apart. After the call, Chelsea tried her hardest to focus back on her editing with no luck. Casey left Monica and had served her divorced papers. Chelsea wondered what prompted that after all these years. She

shouldn't even let it concern her. She could bet
Monica wouldn't care less if their positions were
reversed, but she knew divorce wasn't easy on
anyone.

Walking over to the club entrance, she
noticed the line full of people trying to get in. Several
peopled eyed her skeptically as she passed them and
complained when the bouncer let her in. She ignored
it. She was coming to work. The other bouncer let her
through security, and she headed to the back hall for
employees only. She shrugged her coat off, tossing it
in the cubic before heading over to the bar. The
music was at full blast. Tables were full, bodies were
dancing, and the lights were circling around. She
made it to the bar, looking for Josh, and was
surprised to see Jacen working work alongside Josh
taken orders. When he looked up, he was just as
surprised to see her as she was to see him.

"What are you doing here?" he shouted for
her to hear him over the music.

"Josh called for the calvary." she said
jokingly. Jacen's head whipped over to Josh.

"What?" he shouted. "We need help." he
continued. Jacen blew out a breath.

"Add one more debt to the pile." he said.

"At this point, you'll owe me forever." she joked, but Jacen made a face she couldn't make out. He quickly recovered when the music change, and Chelsea wondered what thought had crossed his mind."

"Kyra is struggling with VIP orders." He announced. She nodded, grabbed an extra shirt behind the bar, threw it over her head, and asked for two bottles with sparklers. Jacen raised a brow but grabbed them for her.

"They didn't order this." he yelled over the crowd getting loud with the music.

"I have to find some way to get through the crowd." she shouted back. He smiled and placed the sparklers on the bottles as she lit them. Leaving behind the bar, the crowd parted and cheered as she made her way to the VIP section across from the bar. She saw the look of gratitude the moment Kyra laid eyes on her. She mouthed a thank you, and Chelsea smiled and nodded while telling the VIP guest the bottles were on the house. She stayed in the VIP section helping Kyra while Jacen, Josh, and two other waitresses helped the main floor. Time flew past, and it was after four am before she made it back home.

~~~~~~~~~~~~~~~~~~~~~~~

Jacen ran a frustrated hand down his face as he heard the doorbell ring for the third time. He picked up his phone, noticing the time read 10:15 am. Who was at his door? All of his family knew how late he stayed at the club so they wouldn't show up unannounced. For a second, he considered Chelsea, but Chelsea wasn't the type to show up without calling. Plus, she was at the club until four am this morning with him. The doorbell rang again, and he almost growled. Throwing the covers off in aggravation, he did his best not to stomp. He finally made it to his front door and opened it. This time he growled.

"What are you doing here, Lauren?"

"Well, good morning to you too." She said smirkingly. Leaning on the door, Jacen ran another frustrating hand down his face.

"What do you want?" he asked.

"I think it's time we talked."

"We don't have anything to talk about." Jacen stated flatly.

"Are you sure about that?" She asked.

"Pretty sure. Now, if you don't mind, it's cold, and I'm going back to bed." He straightened his stance in hopes of closing the door.

"Even if it means saving the new location for your club?"

"What are you talking about?"

"Let me in, and I'll tell you."

"Tell me, and I'll think about letting you in." Jacen countered. A not-so-nice breeze decided to blow past, sending a chill up Jacen's bare legs. Frustrated and practically freezing, he stepped aside, allowing Lauren in. The moment he closed the door, he saw her attempt to unbutton her coat.

"Don't get comfortable. Say whatever it is you came here to say so I can get back to sleep." Not expecting his rejection, she looked at him shocked, her fingers left the buttons, and she folded her arms.

"You're not seriously dating Chelsea Stone, are you?" She seethed. Jacen folded his arms, matching her stance.

"My relationship with Chelsea is not up for discussion. You said you have some information about the new location; what is it?"

"Well, you dating Chelsea is a part of it."

"I can't possibly see how the two are related." Jacen responded. Lauren unfolded her arms and began to step toward him.

"It's simple. If you stop dating Chelsea and take me to the Charity Ball, I'll save the club for you."

"Lauren, what are you talking about?"

"The city is planning to tear down the building you want for your new club." His stance lightened that was news to him.

"How did you find that out?

"You know my uncle is friends with the commissioner. I overheard him discussing a new land developer here in Boston." Her answer didn't sit well with him. Not only was she telling him he was potentially losing the location for the second club, but that the city was making negotiations with a new land developer. A contract that his older brother Justin currently held. He would have to talk with Justin later. Right now, he had an unwanted guest to get rid of.

"Let me get this straight. You're offering to stop a potential demolition on the new location if I dump Chelsea and take you to the Charity ball."

"It's an arrangement that gets us what we both want." Her body was practically plastered against his. "It just depends. How much the new location means to you?" She added. It wasn't a secret that he planned to expand. Most of the investors in Boston didn't want to invest in another nightclub. He had yet to hear back from his father's friend from Texas. But blackmail wasn't his thing.

"I think you're asking the wrong question here, Lauren?" He asked in a low voice.

"And what question should I be asking?" She asked, attempting a seductive tone. He leaned down close enough for their noses to almost touch and looked directly into her eyes. Her eyes focused on his, shifted to his lips, as if expecting a kiss.

"How much does Chelsea mean to me?" He saw the instant his words and their meaning hit her. She quickly stepped back, and a murderous gaze starred back at him.

"You would give up a chance at saving the new location for her?" She sniped. He honestly knew

Chelsea meant more to him than getting into cahoots with Lauren again. Whether she really had the power to convince her uncle to stop the demolition or not, he didn't want to be involved with her anyway, but thinking over her questions. Yes, he would give up the new location for Chelsea. If he had to, he'd give up a whole lot more. Seeing the revelation of his feelings unfolding right before Lauren, he halted any further conversation with her and asked her to leave. She ranted and complained, but he closed the door ignoring her slight tantrum, and headed back to his bed. He was far from sleepy, although he knew he needed to rest. Finally, back in his bed, he thought about the conversation with Lauren. If the demolition took place, he would have to start finding another spot for a second location. But none of it trumped him, realizing he was in love with Chelsea Stone.

Chapter Seventeen

"You are so lucky that I love you." Chelsea said, plopping down in the booth where Ashiree was already sitting looking at the menu. They always chose the back booth as their Saturday morning breakfast spot.

"What's got your panties in a wad this morning?" Ashiree asked. Chelsea almost groaned. She was operating on less than five hours of sleep.

"I'm just tired, that's all."

"Another late-night editing?" Ashiree asked.

"No, I actually was helping Jacen at the club last night until after four this morning."

"Why so late? I thought you mainly helped with the diner."

"I do, but last night Jacen was shorthand." Chelsea explained.

"Jacen seriously needs to start paying you." Ashiree stated. Chelsea chuckled.

"I don't mind helping."

"You are beyond helping at this point."

"I honestly needed the distraction. Being alone in my brownstone, left to my own thoughts, isn't good."

"Why? What happened?" Ashiree asked, sipping her coffee.

"Casey is divorcing Monica." Chelsea responded, causing Ashiree to nearly choke on her coffee.

"What? When did you find this out?"

"Sonica called me. She and Nigel returned from their honeymoon to family chaos." Chelsea explained. She watched Ashiree recover from choking and waited for her response.

"Have you heard from Casey?" Ashiree asked. Chelsea shook her head. "Do you want to hear from Casey?" She continued. Chelsea pondered on Ashiree's question; she hadn't considered it before. Casey was a part of her past. Did she really want to go back? To see what could have been. Of course, this was based on if Casey would seek her out. During the wedding, he seemed very eager to speak with her. And what about Jacen? Their six weeks were almost up. She also heard rumors he was still seeing Lauren. She didn't want to believe them.

"I don't know Ashiree." She answered
honestly. The waitress took their order, brought
Chelsea her hot chocolate, and refiled Ashiree's
coffee cup. Chelsea was about to ask Ashiree a
question when the booth in front of them seated new
customers, and Chelsea recognized one of their
voices.

"Why do you look so tired?" one voice asked.

*"I just left Jacen's. You know how insufferable
he can be?"*

"Jacen's? As in Jacen Turner."

"Of course, who else?"

*"Wow. I thought the two of you were over
since he's been all over Boston with Chelsea Stone."*

*"He has not been all over Boston. He's just
doing the calendar events with her."*

"Is he still taking her to the charity ball?"

*"Yes, we've discussed it. He can't just ditch
her because things are back on with us."*

"I don't know, Lauren."

"What do you mean?"

*"Everyone knows how close Chelsea is with
the Turner family, especially Shayna Masters-Turner.*

The gossip mills are speculating she is the next Turner wife."

"Psst. Please. There is no way Jacen would ever marry Chelsea Stone."

Chelsea slouched down in her seat after overhearing the conversation between Lauren and her friend. Ashiree nudged her foot under the table and eyed her to rebuttal Lauren's words, but she shook her head. The waitress returned with their food, and honestly, Chelsea lost her appetite. They ate in silence, or at least Ashiree did, and stayed seated in the booth until long after Lauren and her friend left. Chelsea stayed lost in her thoughts. Her mind whirled through the last five weeks with Lauren's words. Was she wrong in believing things between her and Jacen were actually progressing? Had she read the signs all wrong? The waitress brought Chelsea another hot chocolate, adding extra marshmallows at Ashiree's request for her. Chelsea managed a slight smile to the waitress in a thank you and noticed Ashiree watching her. She didn't speak, only nodded for Chelsea to drink the hot chocolate. Moments like this, she loved her best friend. Ashiree understood when Chelsea just needed someone present while she collected her thoughts or needed time to process.

~~~~~~~~~~~~~~~~~~~~~~~

Lauren sat in her car across from the restaurant with a slight smirk on her face. She could admit that Jacen's continuous rejection of her advances stung in ways she'd never experience. He hadn't actually told her no to the possibility of taking her to the Charity Ball. She didn't care if he had feelings for Chelsea, which just baffled her. Chelsea Stone, the quiet girl that wasn't even brave enough to admit she had feelings for Jacen. How they came together for the calendar events to begin with, she would never understand. But Chelsea wasn't a fighter, and Lauren wanted Jacen to see that Chelsea wasn't the best woman for him. She so easily caused doubt in Chelsea's gullible mind. The opportunity could not have worked out better when she saw Chelsea sitting in the booth with her friend. Chelsea was plain and ordinary even with her bi-racial features. Ashiree, however, could put up some serious competition if she wanted. Luckily for Lauren, her rival was Chelsea, the passive one. The one that didn't speak up for herself. The girl that would rather hang out and work for the man she had a crush on, than actually step up to the plate and go for him. Not that Lauren believed she had any real chance of snagging Jacen Turner. But Jacen needed a woman by his side who was bold and could handle the pressure of being married into a very respected and prominent family in Boston. And that woman was not Chelsea Stone. Even if Jacen decided to continue, what she knew as a poorly played charade, he would move on after the calendar. But if he agreed to her terms, he could have the best woman by his side and get the one thing he truly wished for. Smiling again, Lauren continued to watch Chelsea, looking down into her cup, tracing the rim of it with her finger in deep thought. Lauren could help the pride at the distress she caused. Chelsea Stone was no match for her, and she wasn't a good match for Jacen.

~~~~~~~~~~~~~~~~~~~~~~~~

"Are you sure you heard her correctly?"

"Pretty sure." Jacen responded to his brother's question. After finally getting a few hours of sleep once Lauren left his townhouse, he showered, got dressed, and headed back to the club. On the way to the club, he'd called his brother Justin regarding

Lauren's statement about the city having a new land developer. He continued to listen as Justin explained he'd get in contact with congressman Taylor, who was Trent's father, to see if there was any truth to Lauren's words. He also informed Jacen that he would check the city's list of scheduled demolitions to see if the new location was on it. Jacen thanked his brother and ended the call. He was a little surprised when arrived at Ensconce and Heidi informed him Chelsea wasn't coming in. He'd texted her, but she hadn't responded. Jacen shrugged it off, assuming she was probably still asleep. Last night had only added to the stress he was already under. Somehow two parties had been booked for the VIP section, and neither group had been happy for the oversite. By trying to accommodate both parties, with the club maxed to capacity, he shouldn't have been surprised that Josh had called Chelsea. He prayed tonight's crowd would be more manageable.

Resting back in his office desk chair, he heard the ding on his phone, indicating he had an email. Checking it, he saw an invitation to confirm his attendance to the Charity Ball. Had it been almost six weeks already? Hitting accept, he placed the phone down and rubbed his hand down his face. His time with Chelsea was almost up. If he were honest with himself, he wanted things with them to continue and not under the pretense of a fake relationship. Most of their time together centered around being at the diner or the events for the calendar. He'd only taken her on two dates, and dinner with his family.

He'd come so close to kissing her after he tackled her in the snow. The kiss he was finally ready to indulge in again was shamelessly interrupted but his sister-in-law. He half chuckled at the warning look Shayna gave him, while also slightly annoyed about Shayna stopping him from kissing Chelsea, but he honestly wasn't surprised. All the Turner wives were protective of her in some way, and if he added Ashiree to the mix, the four corners of hell would erupt on him if he hurt her.

~~~~~~~~~~~~~~~~~~~~

Chelsea arrived home as she noticed a black SUV parked in front of her Brownstown. She smiled, thinking Jacen was waiting for her. They hadn't talked much in the last couple of days, a few texts here and there, but they hadn't seen each other. He'd hired two new staff members for the club and hadn't needed to help in the diner or club. Her smile faded as she realized the occupant in the truck wasn't Jacen; it was Casey. He shivered and gripped his coat as he approached her.

"How do you manage to live in this cold weather?" He said.

"Casey, what are you doing here?" She asked, ignoring his comment about the cold. It actually wasn't a bad day to be in the second week of November.

"We need to talk?" She lifted an eyebrow. "Please Chelsea?" She eyed him more skeptically. She could admit she'd felt sorry for the situation with Monica, but that didn't mean she wanted him to believe he could come to her.

"Not here." She stated. She wasn't letting Casey in her home.

"At long as it gets me out of this cold. I don't care." She nodded, and he opened the back door of the SUV. She hadn't realized the vehicle was still on and a driver was waiting for them. She gave the driver directions to a small cafe not too far from her home. Arriving a few minutes later, Casey and Chelsea found a seat in the back.

"This is nice. Quite cozy." He said, rubbing his hands together and quickly ordering a cup of coffee. She ordered a hot chocolate and waited for the waitress to retreat. There weren't many people around, and she was thankful for that. She had no idea how this conversation was going to go.

"It is pretty cozy, but let's cut to the reason you're here." She says plainly.

"I miss this side of you." He said with a slight smile. She leaned back in her chair and stared at him.

"I'm divorcing Monica." He stated as if he was still coming to grips with his decision.

"I heard."

"We need to talk about what happened with us." He said, almost pleading.

"It was a long time ago, Casey. I'm over it."

"Are you?" He asked. She almost answered a resounding yes, but the waitress came by with their drinks. Casey quickly wrapped his hands around his cup and closed his eyes. She tried not to laugh as she watched him sigh while he heated his hands up with his cup.

"You're so overdramatic," she said.

"I literally cannot feel my fingers tip." She chuckled and took a sip of her hot chocolate. Casey finally decided to take a sip of his coffee.

"Why do we need to talk about what happened with us, Casey?" He took another sip of his coffee and made eye contact with her.

"Because I thought you betrayed me, Chelsea."

"What are you talking about?"

"I saw you with Steven."

"What?"

"At the boathouse, at our spot. His arm was around you." He probably had seen them, but she'd been stupidly crying over him.

"I never did anything, Steven."

"I thought you did."

"Why would you think that? Huh? To ease your guilt about sleeping with Monica."

"It was all a lie, Chelsea." He said tensely but kept his tone low.

"No, it wasn't. I saw you kissing Monica, and she was all too happy to tell me how you'd chose her over me, how everything you did and said to make me feel special, you also did for her."

"It wasn't true. I didn't do any of those things with her." The eighteen-year-old girl in her wanted to believe him. But what good could any of that information do for her now?

"It doesn't matter, Casey. As I said, it was a long time ago. I'm over it." And she meant it. Maybe knowing things were orchestrated against them at the hand of Monica helped him in some way free himself from her clutches, but Monica had done far worse to her than sabotage things with Casey while she was growing up.

"It could have been us that ended up married." He said softly.

"No." she said, shaking her head. If he'd truly wanted her, loved her like he'd claimed, he never would have believed she'd betray him. He never would have let Monica's lies convince him, and he never would have chosen to marry Monica under any circumstances. She watched him nod slowly as if accepting her words and indeed coming to terms with how things worked out. The waitress returned, offering refills, and they both accepted. She didn't say anything as Casey seemed in a daze with his thoughts. Her heart went out to him. It couldn't have been easy to find out you were lied to or manipulated. No one deserves that.

"What will you do now?" She asked, breaking the silence.

"Live." He said with a half-smile. "Me and Sadie might sail for a few months."

"That sounds nice." Chelsea replied. She recalled Casey telling her as a teenager, how much he enjoyed sailing. He even bragged about his father buying him his first yacht at eighteen.

"What about you? Are still with the boyfriend? What's his name again?" He asked teasingly. She laughed because he knew Jacen's name.

"You know his name is Jacen."

"Ah, that's it, Jacen, kind of hard to forget with Garrett still singing his praises." She tried not to laugh at Casey's dry humor.

"We're, okay?"

"Just, okay?" He asked. Chelsea shrugged, not knowing what else to say.

"Honestly, when I decided to come here, I was afraid you'd have a ring on your finger." She quirked a brow at him.

"Why?"

"Because he loves you." Casey stated flatly.

"What?" She answered. Casey thought Jacen loved her? She wished.

"I'm surprised he hasn't told you yet." Casey said, and she shrugged again, not knowing what to say. Jacen hadn't told her that he loved her because he didn't. Not wanting to think about it, she asked about his brothers changing the topic. They talked a while longer as Casey told her how Tommie was working to convince Lorelai to give him a real chance. Apparently, they hooked up at Sonica's wedding. Lorelai was comfortable with the arrangement of a one-night stand, but Tommie was hooked, wanting to change the terms of the agreement.

Casey paid for their drinks, and they exited the cafe. Chelsea laughed at some of the things Tommie was doing to prove to Lorelai he was serious.

"I swear I had to talk him out of kidnapping her until she agreed." Casey joked as they approached his SUV. Chelsea turned and pointed her finger in Casey's chest.

"Don't you let him kidnap my friend." She warned. Casey grabbed her hand and kissed her knuckles, surprising her.

"Anything for you, Chelly." He said with a teasing smirk. She eyed him skeptically and allowed him to assist her into his SUV.

"No more flirting, Casey Worthington." She said as she settled in her seat, and he closed the door.

"You can't blame a guy for trying." He said, and she playfully scowled at him. He threw his head back, laughing, and put his hands upon mock surrender. Then instructed his driver to take her home.

Chapter Eighteen

Jacen was leaving downtown and heading back home after attending a city council meeting. Somehow Justin had managed to get them an impromptu meeting with the permit committee. After hearing Lauren's uncle planned to bring in a new developer and ignore the city's construction contract with JAT construction, Justin's company. He discovered a few projects going on within the city that had not been given to his company. The meeting lasted two hours. The upside was Justin was now issued the contracts on the three projects the city hadn't realized were not contracted with his company. The downside is that the permit with the new locations club was being held. Jacen knew it was a power move by Lauren's uncle. He'd been embarrassed and slightly reprimanded for not abiding by the contract the city had with Justin's company. But he knew Jacen wanted the club, and in pure treacherous form, he held back the permit, saying some zoning issues needed to be addressed. Jacen wanted to call bs, but Justin told him to wait for it. Jacen was detoured off the freeway due to construction and ended up seeing a flower shop. He smiled as he pulled over. He hadn't bought Chelsea flowers yet. It was one of the things he wanted to do for her. She'd never received flowers before, and he wanted to be her first. Entering the flower shop, the cashier happily smiled and greeted him. He explained that he wanted to get flowers for his girlfriend. She smiled at him, suggesting an array of bouquets with roses and tulips. He'd purchased roses before, mainly for his mother but also for a couple of women in his past. He'd never bought tulips before. He smiled, choosing the tulips. It would be a first for him and Chelsea. He thanked the cashier as she rang up his order and boxed the tulips. He headed out of the shop and was almost to his truck when he heard someone laugh. But not just anyone. Chelsea. He turned and saw her walking out of a cafe with a guy. His first emotion was curiosity, wondering who she was with and what they were laughing about. His next emotions were both shock and surprise when the profile of the man's face became clear. Casey? What was Casey doing in Boston? The last two emotions he felt, he hated to admit to himself. Jealousy and anguish stirred inside of him as he watched Casey take Chelsea's hand and kiss her knuckles. She didn't even snatch away. She only smiled and gotten in the SUV. His phone vibrated in his pocket, breaking his stare of the vehicle pulling off. He felt like an idiot holding a box of flowers for her, thinking of the expression she would have once she saw them. He had half a mind to toss the flowers. He pulled his phone from his pocket to check his message. One from Josh confirmed the lineup for Amateur night, and as he responded to Josh, another one from Shayna came through, reminding him of the last photo shoot before the Charity ball. He almost dreaded answering he'd be there. He headed to his townhouse, failed to get a good nap, and frustratingly took a shower and headed to the club. The entire time trying to get the image of Chelsea and Casey out of his head.

~~~~~~~~~~~~~~~~~~~~~~

Chelsea informed Heidi she was heading downstairs to the club before she left. She purposely came to help with the diner today. She needed to talk to Jacen. After her talk with Casey, she allowed herself to see her relationship differently. Although Casey flirted with her the entire ride back to her house, in all sincerity, he told her he was happy for her. But teased her, stating if things didn't work out, he'd be there to help her mend her broken heart. She laughed at his teasing and told him to focus more on Lorelai and Tommie. She had accepted from the beginning that suffering a broken heart would be an inevitable fate for her once things were over with calendar events. But she'd felt hopeful that maybe Casey had seen something that she hadn't. He was a guy, and guys knew what other guys were feeling, right? Either way, her quick dash of hope was faltered by Jacen's lack of communication in the last couple of days. She and Ashiree both attended the return of Amateur Night. The club was packed, and tickets were sold out. The local talent nailed it joke for joke, and she couldn't remember laughing so hard. She noticed Jacen standing in the back next to the bar during one of the comedians' acts, she smiled at him, but he hadn't smiled back, after the show she went to find him in his office only to be told he was in a meeting with a talent scout. She didn't let that bother her at first. She knew bringing back Amateur night was a way to help local comedians get exposed, but now three days later, she still hadn't heard a word from him. She didn't understand it. The charity ball was this weekend. She'd already bought a dress that she looked forward to wearing, hoping that he would be pleased. A gripping fear of the rumors with Laurens being true, hit her. They hadn't discussed the charity ball. Were they going to ride together? Did he even plan on picking her up? She needed to know.

Heading to the back stairs where his office was, she noticed his door looked closed. She thought about retreating, maybe he was busy, but something nagged her that perhaps he was upset with her or, worse, done with her. If he were, he'd have to tell her to her face. It would hurt like a knife to the heart, but she wouldn't have to worry any longer or allow her thoughts to think they could ever have a chance of being together. She knocked on his door with her knuckle. He looked up from his desk and the smile that generally appeared on his face when he saw her was nowhere to be found.

"Hey." she said in a shaking breath.

"Hi." he said before looking back down at the papers on his desk. She was mildly startled by the frosty tone of his voice. He wouldn't even look at her. Chelsea could feel tears wanting to spring in her eyes, but she willed them back. She knew from the beginning that this was never permanent. That things between them were never real, no matter how much she wanted them to be.

"I haven't heard from you." she mustered up the courage to say. She heard him inhale a long breath as if talking to her was the last thing he wanted to do.

"I've been busy." he answered dryly. And the tears welled up. His words and demeanor felt cold, harsh, and unwelcoming. What happened? What had she missed? He must have noticed she hadn't said anything, because he finally decided to look up at her, and the moment he did, the tears fell.

"Chelsea." he began. She shook her head. She didn't want him to say anything else.

"I'm sorry, I bothered you." she said and ran from his office. He called her name a few times, but she kept going. She grabbed her coat and scarf and left out the back door without even putting her coat on.

~~~~~~~~~~~~~~~~~~~~~~~~

Jacen made it out the back door of the diner just as Chelsea's car pulled out into the street. He rubbed his hand down his face feeling every bit of the jerk he was. He hurt her. He wasn't trying to, but he had. He struggled the last few days trying to remove the image of Chelsea and Casey from his mind and failed. He couldn't look at her. It hurt to look at her. By his own stupidity, he actually googled Casey Worthington, and with all the news, media, and press about him, the main article that caught his attention was the one announcing he was divorcing his wife. Chelsea's sister. He knew why Casey has been in Boston. He wanted Chelsea. The two of them laughing coming out of the cafe, Casey kissing her knuckles, Chelsea's reluctance to push him away solidified Jacen had lost her. And then he had to laugh at himself because, in all honesty, he hadn't had her. She didn't want to be a fling for him. She tried to protect her image while doing the calendar events, and he respected it. But she also admitted she didn't want to be considered as the next Turner wife. He was just a friend that she was helping out. A favor for a favor. Leave it to him to fall for the one woman that didn't want him back. It hurt to even know that. It hurt to know how much everyone liked her, and she genuinely liked them, but he loved her, and she didn't love him back. Women he'd dated in the past moved on to the next conquest as he had. It hadn't bothered him one bit, but with Chelsea? The thought of Chelsea being with someone else hurt in in ways he couldn't even explain. The thought of her being with Casey almost crushed his heart. He knew they had history, even knew Casey was her first. Didn't the saying go 'you always love your first? And now, with Monica out of the picture, what was stopping them. Obviously, nothing. His and Chelsea's relationship was supposed to be over after this weekend. But it didn't change the fact that even if she were choosing to be with Casey, she didn't deserve his rudeness, no matter what. It wasn't her fault that he had fallen for her, that he planned to tell her at the charity ball that he didn't want them to be over. She wasn't responsible for his feelings or his actions.

Walking back into the building and back down the stairs, he saw one of the bouncers standing by his door.

"Is everything alright?" it wasn't, but Jacen didn't feel like telling him that. He nodded, and then went over to the security detail for that night. He'd hired a few new people to secure the parking lot, and he wanted to make sure they were ready. After talking with the club staff, he checked on Heidi as she was closing the diner soon. She looked at him and answered him curtly, knowing full well what had happened with him and Chelsea's encounter. The other servers and cooks kept busy pretending to be indifferent to the situation. But Jacen knew better. These were people who liked Chelsea, worked with her, laughed with her, and felt protective of her. He thought about waiting to talk to her tomorrow, but waiting wasn't the best decision. He spoke with Josh and let him know to call him if anything went wrong, Josh nodded, and Jacen closed up his office and left.

~~~~~~~~~~~~~~~~~~~~~~~~~

"I should seriously kick you in the balls." Chelsea heard Ashiree say as she answered the door.

"I would hope you wouldn't do that." Chelsea gasped at hearing Jacen's voice.

"Give me one good reason why I shouldn't?" Ashiree countered.

"I can give you a reason, but I'm not sure if you'll think it's a good one." Jacen answered. Chelsea stood from the couch with her blanket to walk to the edge of the foyer. Ashiree was standing in her doorway, poking her finger in Jacen's chest.

"I told you not to hurt her." Ashiree warned. She watched Jacen's words die on his lips as he looked over Ashiree and saw her.

"I didn't mean to." he said, his eyes still fixed at her. Ashiree turned around, noticing her in the foyer.

"Am I kneeing him in the balls or letting him in?" Chelsea saw Jacen slightly flinch at Ashiree's words.

"Let him in." she answered softly and almost recognized a thank you expression on Jacen's' face.

"Hi." he said, coming to stand in front of her.

"You better have a better make line than that." she heard Ashiree say after closing the front door. Chelsea smiled, watching Ashiree walk past them into the living room and grabbed her coat and purse.

"I'll catch up with you later." she said, putting on her coat and coming to kiss Chelsea on the cheek before turning to Jacen. "You get one more chance, and that's only because I honestly like you. But don't mess up again." Ashiree said, pointing her finger at him in another warning before leaving the brownstone. Chelsea looked back up at Jacen.

"What are you doing here?"

"I came to apologize. I shouldn't have been so rude to you earlier."

"You didn't have to come all the way over here to apologize. You could have texted." she said, stepping back from him and turning to have a seat on her couch. He watched her sit and placed his hands in his pockets.

"You would want me to text you an apology?"

"It would be the most communication I've had with you in the last three days." she said. His face fell in slight embarrassment. She didn't want to make this hard, and she didn't want to cry anymore.

"I had my reasons." he said quietly. She nodded, not wanting to feel the pain of his words. The band-aid was just slowly being pulled off.

"Look, you don't have to say it. I know it was never going to be real between us. I just would have liked for you to have let me know before you moved on to someone else." She couldn't look at him while she spoke. The very thought that he was with Lauren, hurt her. She couldn't even hold his attention for six weeks.

"I could say the same thing to you." He said, breaking her thoughts. She jerked her head up at his tone. His face varied with emotions of pain, anger, and hurt. What was he hurt about?

"How could you say the same thing?" she asked, utterly confused.

"Because you're just now telling me you believe things were never going be real between us? You didn't think to tell me that before now? Before you moved on."

"What are you talking about? I haven't talked to you in days?"

"Is that what you would have told me had you talked to me? That we were over." he looked so hurt. How could he look so hurt? She was the one hurting.

"No, but it seems you should have."

"It wasn't over to me, Chelsea." Jacen stated a tense edge in his voice.

"Then why have you not spoken to me in three days." she yelled, standing up from the couch.

"Because I saw you with Casey." he yelled back at her, shocking her.

Chapter Nineteen

Jacen rubbed his hand down his face, regaining his composure, he hadn't meant to yell, but he loved her; he loved so much it hurt. And he'd lost her.

"What?" he had her say in a shaken breathe.

"I saw you with Casey." he said softly.

"Jacen…"

"It's okay." he began as he walked over to stand in front of her. Looking at her tear-stained cheeks from how harsh he'd been with her earlier. He cupped her face, resting his forehead on hers and inhaling her sweet scent. This was the hardest goodbye he would have in his life. He thought giving up on his infatuation with Alexia was hard. And that's precisely what it had been, infatuation, intrigue, but never love. He knew the difference because back then, his pride, his feelings were geared more to some sort of competition he'd lost. Now, he was losing his heart. He'd lost it, and he knew no other woman would have it.

"It's not okay." she said.

"It is, I promise." He tried to reassure. She shook her head, and he felt tears etch the side of his fingers. "Baby, don't cry." he continued, allowing the endearment to slip from his lips before he could stop it. He slowly began kissing her tears away. "I'm sorry I yelled."

"I yelled too." she admitted. He lifted his head, and she opened her teary eyes to meet his.

"Jacen..." she began, but he kissed the word from her lips. He didn't want her rejection or explanation of her feelings not reflecting his own. He kissed her softly, sweetly, lovingly. She moaned and cried against his lips, and he took her mouth urgently, expressing every desire, want, and need he had for her. Wishing he could make her his, wishing he acted sooner. Claiming her, marking her, making love to her, showing in every way that she belonged with him. As breathing became a necessity, every muscle in his body ached to have to pull away. He began to drop his hands from her face, finally accepting he had to let her go. His fingers grazed her cheek as they slowly descended. As his hands reached her chin, she caught and stopped them from falling by cupping them with her own.

"Jacen." she said, and his heart almost broke knowing he'd never heard her say his name like that again. He allowed his eyes to meet hers. "I'm not with Casey." He stopped breathing and blinked a few times before he finally exhaled, hearing her words.

"What?" he was barely able to say. She smiled in his palms.

"I'm not with Casey." she said slowly, allowing him to catch every word.

"But I saw you."

"When?"

"Last week, leaving the cafe, smiling, and he kissed..."

"What you saw as a very much needed goodbye." Chelsea said.

"A goodbye?"

"Yes, a goodbye." She confirmed.

"But he's divorcing Monica."

"Yes, he is." she said.

"He didn't come here for you?"

"He did, but as you can see, he's not here now."

"Then why did you think we were over?

"Again, you haven't been talking to me." she said in a teasing manner, and he couldn't help but chuckle. He'd read it all wrong. He'd spent the last three days in complete torment, thinking she wanted Casey. "Not to mention the whole Lauren situation."

"What Lauren situation?" He asked, puzzled.

"Lauren is apparently telling people that you are taking her to the charity ball and dumping me." Chelsea answered.

"What?"

"Yes, she says, you two have some sort of arrangement and that you are trying to let me down easy."

"And me not talking to you made you believe it." He stated. He'd been a bigger jerk than he'd thought.

"I didn't want to think you'd do that to me, but I can't say the thought hadn't crossed my mind."

"Baby, I'm so sorry. And trust me, I do not have an agreement with Lauren."

"Why does she think that you do?"

"Let's sit down, and I'll tell you everything later. Right now, I just want to hold you, kiss you, and make you mine."

The ballroom at the governor's mansion was immaculately decorated in Christmas-themed decor. The chandelier in the opening foyer shined brightly over the room as Boston's most prominent and influential attendees began to arrive. Chelsea gripped Jacen's arms a little tighter as he walked them over to their table. They were stopped and confronted by several businessmen and women that Chelsea did not know, but she was grateful to see the Turner wives in attendance, and they were seated at the table nearest her and Jacen's.

"Chelsea, you look beautiful." Kaycee Turner said as she greeted them. Chelsea chose a coral cream floral-length gown. Sheer straps laced her shoulder and her hair cascaded down in a massive wave of curls down her back.

"Thank you. You each look lovely yourselves." she said, taking the time to notice the elegant gowns worn by the other women. Shayna said her greeting then politely stole Jacen away. Kaycee and Alexia excused themselves as Chelsea watched them go stand beside their husbands. Finding her seat, she nodded, and greeted the few people sitting around her table. She found Jacen talking to few sponsors and could admit he looked calm and well put together.

A server appeared, and she gladly accepted the champagne and ordered a glass of Chardonnay for Jacen. She smiled, remembering him taking her to the wine tasting. She hadn't known how much he enjoyed it until then. Taking a sip of her champagne, she took in the room around her. She wished Ashiree had decided to attend. Her friend did not like the spotlight, or more so, she didn't like large crowds of people. Conversation with strangers was never a strong suit for either of them. They were alike in that sense. But Chelsea had been hiding in plain sight mostly all of her life.

"Sorry about that." Jacen said, slightly startling her. She hadn't heard him approach the table. He took his seat just as the server returned with the glass of wine. Jacen lifted a brow while accepting the drink.

"The lady ordered for you, sir." The waiter explained.

"Thank you." Jacen said as the server turned to another table to deliver another drink. Chelsea watched as Jacen did a slight swerve with his glass, inhaled the scent of the wine before taking a sip.

"That is a good Chardonnay." he remarked. "How did you know?" he asked Chelsea.

"I remember you talking about it with the winemaker." She answered.

"You paid attention. I truly thought you were bored." Jacen teased.

"No, not at all. Surprised for sure. A lot of time goes into a good bottle of wine."

"Very true." he replied, looking at her over the rim of his wine glass as he took another sip. The heat in his gaze stirred a rising desire in her.

An attendee interrupted her thoughts and Jacen's gaze shifted as they approached the table to speak with Jacen. Chelsea decided to take a sip from her flute to calm her nerves. Shayna soon took the podium and began to welcome and thank everyone for attending. She expressed her appreciation of those continuing to support the charity event and Calendar, reminding everyone again of how the proceeds were distributed and the need to continue the cause. Chelsea felt Jacen scoot a little closer to her and reached for her hand under the table. She plastered on the best smile she could as Shayna remarked how much she enjoyed working with Chelsea again. A few applauds were in the crowd as they looked over at her and Jacen. She smiled up at Shayna, also pleased to have worked with her again. Reminiscing on all the crazy deadlines and late nights at Show Stoppin.

~~~~~~~~~~~~~~~~~~~~~~

   Jacen couldn't help but feel the slight shudder from Chelsea's hand as Shayna reminisced and praised her time with Chelsea in front of all of Boston. He loved his sister-in-law more than he ever thought he could at that moment. She had pulled him to the side, ready to scold him about a rumor she'd heard about him and Lauren. He should not have been surprised. Lauren had twisted the situation of her showing up at his house a couple of weeks back. Shayna was livid when he told her the truth, especially Lauren's uncle's part in stopping the permit on the building he wanted. He knew Shayna's speech right now was to correct any slander against Chelsea's name and confirming him and Chelsea's relationship. One that would continue after this evening and long into the future. After the misunderstanding over Casey, he knew there was no going back. He wanted Chelsea in his life. It didn't matter if they were cleaning up the bar, serving in the diner, sharing a cookie in the park, wearing ridiculous costumes for a photoshoot, or laying in each other's arms while watching a movie; he wanted it all. And he wanted it with her. The last two months seemed to fly by, but he'd made so many memories with Chelsea in that time. If, in six weeks, he could share and learn so much, what would six months do? Six years, sixty years? He wanted to find out. He wanted a life with Chelsea. The uncomfortable family gatherings, mainly on her end, snowball fights with random kids, stargazing at night on the pier, listening to her talk about the latest book she'd edited, explaining the rules of football to her, and teaching her to play pool, he wanted it all.

The crowd began to clap, interrupting his thoughts, as Shayna proudly announced the display of the final calendar photos. Lifting his head toward the descending screen, he watched as well as others as the last photos selected for the Calendar displayed. Picture by picture, various responses came from the crowd. The shots were very good of him and Chelsea.

They photographed very well together, and despite the height difference, they seem to complement each other. He was almost embarrassed at the Halloween costume choice for him and Chelsea as the iconic characters Khal Drogo and Daenerys Targaryen from Game of thrones. He hadn't been a fan of the show, but his chest structure seemed to give Jason Momoa a run for his money. He laughed with others as the November shot came into view and loved that Shayna had chosen a single image of him with the kids at the shelter. Their last shot nearly took his breath away. As tradition would have it, December was always a Santa shot. The hat, no shirt, the pants, and a potential prop of a reindeer. This year Shayna had chosen to do something different. He knew what she had in mind when they'd decided to shoot the walk in the park scene, but he never could have predicted the picture colleague. One, with him and Chelsea running away from the camera crew, the second one, was them meeting the kids and the last was a shot right before Shayna interrupted Jacen kissing Chelsea. He didn't know the camera could get a close-up shot from that far away, but he could see his profile so clearly. His sly smile, loving and adoring, was entirely allured by the sweet and tender smile on Chelsea's face. The clapping around them at the final photo prompted Jacen to look at Chelsea. Her head turned slowly to his, misty tears in her eyes and a sweet smile on her face.

"And now, ladies and gentlemen, I welcome to the stage, this years' Boston Calendar Bachelor, Jacen Turner." He slowly stood nodding to everyone while slowly releasing Chelsea's hand and walking up to the podium. The speech he had prepared left the recesses of his mind. He did his best to thank everyone for coming and encouraging them to purchase the Calendar and continue to donate to other charities the Calendar helped provide services for. He quickly stepped down from the podium while the clapping continued, and Shayna took over. Jacen reached Chelsea and extended his hand, inviting her to come with him. She stood accepting his hand, and they nodded as they passed people congratulating them on the Calendar, expressing their support for them as couples and accolades of this being the best Calendar ever. Jacen was grateful for all of their words, and five months ago, he would have reveled in their praise and admiration of him, but at this moment, he needed Chelsea alone.

Finally making it to the veranda off the ballroom, he quickly pushed her through the double doors and closed them. The moment they had privacy, Jacen promptly brought Chelsea into his arms and latched his mouth onto hers. Taking her mouth with a fierce need and desire. All night, he had been on his best behavior. Since the moment he picked her up, until the moment they arrived, and then sitting next to her viewing the evidence of their six weeks together. Their chemistry, their body language, and last their desire for each other, capture in every photo. He didn't have any more reservations about her feelings or her wants regarding them staying together. It was evident in every picture, every scene, every moment they were together. He broke off their kiss as breathing became necessary. Resting his head on her forehead and allowing himself to breathe in her scent. Jacen felt the slight shudder of her body as he continued to hold her. He loved the feel of her in his arms.

"Chelsea, you mentioned before that you didn't think things could be real between us, but I want this to be as real as it can get. I want us together for as long as you'll have me. I want you to be by my side, in my life, encouraging me when I'm down, cheering me to keep going." he watched a slight blush rose on her cheeks. He smiled." I want you blushing when I compliment you, nervous when I flirt with you, shuddering when I kiss you, and crying out when I make love to you. I want it all Chelsea. I want you to never worry about having a family or being alone. You're practically already in my family." he joked. She chuckled with a tear finally grazing down her cheek. "I want you to always come to me, no matter what it is. I love you, Chelsea. You have completely allured me." He finally stated.

Chapter Twenty

Chelsea finished entering that last of her edits for the fantasy novel she was working on. Leaning back, she thought about the previous week. Grinning like a schoolgirl, she couldn't help the smile on her face stretching from ear to ear. Jacen Turner was hers. It was like a dream come true. His declaration of wanting everything with them to be real was more than she could have imagined.

Closing her laptop, she heard her doorbell rang. Checking the time, she wondered who was at her door. She grabbed her robe tighter around her waist and headed down the stairs.

"Coming!" she said as the doorbell rang again. She opened it to find a very disheveled Jacen on her porch.

"Hey, baby." He said.

"Hey, what are you doing here?" she questioned. She assumed he was at the club tonight.

"They tore it down." was the only answer he gave her.

"Come on in." she said, moving to the side to allow him entry. He entered her home, shoulders slumped, and walked over to her sofa, then sat.

"Do you want anything to drink?"

"Alcohol." he said plainly. She quirked a brow and came to stand beside him.

"You don't drink." she stated, and even if he did, he had an entire bar at Ensconce to drink his fill.

"I know, but I finally understand how people feel when they say they need one." he answered. She nodded, headed over to the kitchen, grabbed a bottle of water and poured a glass of wine. When she walked back over to Jacen, he looked at her rather than the items in her hands. He grabbed the wine glass, and she slightly chuckled. Taking the seat next to him, he took a sip from the wine glass and then looked over at her.

"Better?" she asked him with a slight tease. He shook his head and traded the wine glass for the bottle of water.

"I watched." he announced softly.

"You watched the demolition?" she asked, slightly shocked. He nodded.

"It was like watching a knife to the heart of your dream."

"I'm sorry, Jacen." she said. Her heart went out to him. Remembering how happy he had been when he had taken her to the location. Filled with hope and excitement, only to watch it crumble at his feet.

"A year Chelsea. That's how long I've been trying to make this happen."

"I know." she answered, placing her hand over his that rested in between them on the sofa. "But you can't give up."

"Everything else is outside of the city." he stated. Chelsea nodded in understanding. Jacen didn't just live in Boston; he bled Boston. From every historical fact to every sports team, he was a die-hard Boston fan.

"Well, we'll have to keep looking then."

"We?" he asked curiously.

"Yes, what kind of girlfriend would I be if I did not help out." she said, trying to lighten the mood around them.

"You have done so much for me already, Chelsea. With the diner, the club, and the calendar."

"And I'm going to help you with this too, but there is one condition."

"What? Another family event?" he teased. She shook her head vigorously.

"Absolutely not."

"Then what is it?"

"You can't give up." she said, determined to make him see how serious she was, but also how much she believed in him. She watched him sigh and exhale slowly as if he were contemplating her words. After a few seconds, he nodded and placed the water bottle on the coffee table in front of them.

"You're kind of perfect, you know that Chelsea?" he said, looking over at her.

"I believe that's my line." she said. Jacen lightly chuckled and nodded.

"How about we share it?" Jacen suggested. She smiled, reached over, and brought his face to hers for a kiss.

"I love you." She told him after their kiss. He smiled against her lips.

"I love you too."

Six Months Later

Jacen double checked the last few orders before he took a few days off. He was getting married on Saturday, and a smile appeared on his face that he couldn't help. He never would have guessed eight months ago he would have fallen in love and getting married. It was strange how he wondered where the special woman was in his life, the one he would spend forever with. And low and behold, she's been right up under his nose for the past nine years. A knock on his office door brought his head up from the papers he was looking at.

"Come in." he said. He usually kept his door open, but he wanted to ensure everything was in place before leaving for his honeymoon. Josh stepped through the threshold of the door.

"Hey Jacen." he began. Jacen realized how uncomfortable Josh was calling him Jacen and not Mr. Turner. Josh was managing his club now, and honestly, Jacen didn't care about being called Mr. Turner. It was definitely quite confusing when he was in a room with his father and his brothers.

"What's going on, Josh?"

"There is a Mr. Blake here to see you." Jacen lifted a brow in surprise. Why was Donald Blake here? After the demolition of the building he wanted for the second of his club, he'd given up on the expansion lately, focusing on other things, like his future wife.

"Send him in." Jacen stated. Josh nodded, and Jacen began straightening a few items on his desk. He didn't care what his office looked like most of the time, but it wasn't every day a billionaire from Texas showed up. Jacen was putting a few things in a bottom drawer when he heard footsteps enter the office. Standing to his full height, he expected to see an older gentleman in the doorway of his office and was quite surprised by the young man standing before him.

"Mr. Blake?" He asked, coming from behind his desk and extending his hand. The younger man took it with a slight chuckle.

"I can see you were assuming my grandfather." The man said, shaking Jacen's hand. "I'm not surprised. I'm Dominic Blake."

"It's nice to meet you, Dominic. My father speaks very highly of your grandfather." Jacen stated.

A slight shadow seemed to cast over Dominic's face, but he quickly masked it.

"My grandfather speaks quite highly of your father." Dominic admitted.

"So what do I owe the pleasure of this visit?" Jacen asked, inviting Dominic to take a seat and Jacen sat behind his desk.

"I heard you were looking for a second location for your club." Dominic answered.

"I was." Jacen answered, still feeling a little annoyed he wasn't able to stop the demolition in time. Even the property the building sat on was out of his reach.

"Do you no longer wish to expand?" Jacen thought about Dominic's question. He definitely knew he still wanted a second location for his club, possibly a third one, but he'd placed those thoughts on the back burner the last few months. He had a very special woman he was trying to spend eternity with.

"I still plan to expand to a second location. I'm sure you've heard about the previous one I had in mind." Dominic nodded, then said.

"I might have another option for you. Are you interested?" Jacen's interest piqued.

"Sure."

"Then how about we take a ride?" Dominic suggested.

"Lead the way." Jacen answered. Twenty minutes later, Jacen stood outside a vacant lot.

"What do you think of the site?" Dominic asked.

"I'm impressed." Jacen said. The thought of building a new club hadn't crossed his mind. There are very few areas in the Boston Common area that allowed for new construction.

"You'll need a good architect to help construct the site." Dominic stated. Jacen nodded and smiled. He had the perfect architect in mind.

"How did you come across this place?" Jacen asked.

"Let's just say I have a friend who owns a lot of property throughout the country."

"That's some friend for sure."

"He was happy to help. He has more properties than he knows what to do with. Plus, he'd rather spend most of his time on his ranch than worry about his real estate business. But granddad was a little disturbed to hear the city demolished the building you plan to convert into a club. He's not a man to not keep his word, so he told me to find you a building. The building part was difficult, but honestly, I like the idea of creating something new. Renovation is good, but new construction is best."

"I agree. Thank you, Dominic. And thank your grandfather for me also. I was hoping to meet him. I know my dad extended an invitation to my wedding." Jacen said.

"Yes, I heard that. Congratulations. That's another reason I'm here, apparently. My granddad is unable to attend, and your father extended the invitation to me. I hope you don't mind."

"Not at all. We're more than happy to have you." Jacen answered. Dominic nodded, and they turned to walk toward the SUV Dominic rented. Jacen noticed Dominic about to ask a question just as his phone rang. Dominic huffed a breath at whoever the caller was.

"Girlfriend?" Jacen teased.

"I wish. That would be easier." Dominic said before answering the call. "Yes, Shannon." Jacen heard Dominic say as they entered the back of the SUV and returned to his club.

~~~~~~~~~~~~~~~~~~~~~~~

"Who is ready for their bachelorette party?" Kaycee Turner exclaimed as Ashiree opened the door to Chelsea's brownstone. Alexia and Shayna followed behind Kaycee as she walked in. Chelsea groaned slightly and shook her head. She didn't really care to have a bachelorette party, but Ashiree suggested she needed one and sought the assistance of the Turner wives.

"You ladies don't have to go through all this?" Chelsea said.

"Oh, yes, we do. We are in dire need of a girls' night out." Shayna said.

"We have a girl night out every month, Shayna." Alexia explained.

"True, but that's for relaxation from being a mom and a wife. This is about being a woman needing to let our hair down." Shayna explained.

"You do remember what happened the last time you decided to let your hair down, right?" Kaycee teased. Shayna playfully glared at her.

"There is no way I could get drunk and wind up married to someone I hate, again." Shayna countered. Ashiree tried to hide in her chuckle, but Chelsea couldn't. Her laughter brought the others to do the same. It was a well-known fact that Shayna Turner, then Shayna Masters, did not get along with her now-husband Jerome Turner. They were known to have a feud that lasted almost fifteen years and wound up drunken married in Las Vegas.

"Well, tonight is about Chelsea and officially welcoming her as the newest Turner wife." Alexia said. Chelsea smiled at Alexia's comment and thanked her.

"Are you nervous?" Kaycee asked her.

"Not yet, but I'm sure I will be tomorrow." Chelsea admitted.

"You will be fine, I promise, but tonight we are going to help you enjoy your last night as a single woman." Kaycee boasted. The other ladies cheered just as the doorbell rang.

"I'll get it." Ashiree offered. A few seconds later, Erica Masters and Danyelle Taylor Fields walked in.

"Sorry, we're late. We hit some traffic dropping the kids off to my parents." Danyelle explained. She instantly walked over to hug and congratulate Chelsea. Chelsea couldn't help but admire the beauty of the former supermodel. Erica followed suit, also giving her a hug and congratulating her. The women did not share too many similar features even though they shared the same father.

"Alright, I just confirmed Kaitlyn has officially kicked Trent out, and the mansion is ours." Kaycee told them. They all piled into an awaiting limo and toasted to a night of letting their hair down. A few minutes later, they arrived at the iron gate of Trent and Kaitlyn's home. Kaycee confirmed with Kaitlyn over the phone as they arrived at the gate. The limo drove up the long driveway to park in front of the home. It reminded Chelsea of a smaller version of the house of Mr. Darcy in the movie Pride and Prejudice, the version with Keira Knightly. Kaitlyn proudly stood at the top of the stairs.

"I hope you ladies are ready for a night of fun." she said as they each exited the limo. She met

Chelsea halfway and threw a sash over her that said 'Bride'. "Are you ready?" Kaitlyn asked her.

"As ready as I'm going to be." Chelsea answered, slightly nervous. She had no idea what Kaitlyn planned. Out of all of the women, Kaitlyn had a former reputation as the party girl. She held Chelsea's hand as they entered the home and happily explained the itinerary for tonight's events. Kaitlyn led them all into a parlor, and Chelsea noticed two young ladies sitting on a settee sipping champagne.

"Chelsea, I'd like you to meet the Collie and Coddie; they are cousins of Turner brothers." Chelsea greeted them, remembering Jacen had mentioned the triplet cousins that were studying to become lawyers.

"It's nice to meet you." Chelsea said. The resemblance between them was so identical, Chelsea was sure, she would get them mixed up. They needed name tags.

"It's nice to meet you also. I was surprised to hear Jacen was finally getting married." The cousin she believed was Collie said.

"Yes, I just knew he would hold out until he was forty." The other one said with a smirk.

"I thought there were three of you." Chelsea blurted out before she could stop herself. The two sisters looked at each other and smiled.

"There are, Corrie is on a cruise for a much-needed vacation." The one she guessed was Coddie answered her.

"Let's get ready to party, ladies." Kaitlyn announced as she turned down the lights and turned the music on as two men seem to appear out of nowhere. One dressed as a doctor, and the other dressed as a fireman.

"I cannot believe you ordered male strippers." Kaycee scolded.

"It's a bachelorette party. How do you not have strippers?" Kaitlyn answered. Erica, Shayna, and Danyelle nodded in agreement as they watched the men began to strip.

"I can't believe Trent is allowing you to bring them to the house." Alexia said.

"Who said I told him?" Kaitlyn said, slightly yelling over the music. Shayna and Alexia shook their heads while Chelsea and Ashiree shared a slight laugh. It was going to be an exciting night.

Chapter Twenty-One

"What do you think the girls are doing?" James asked as the men stood around in the Trent's New York penthouse. Trent flew them all to New York in his private jet, proclaiming the best bachelor party the world has ever seen.

"Enjoying the Strippers." Trent said, pouring each of them a glass of whiskey.

"You let Kaitlyn bring strippers to your house?" Donovan asked.

"She thinks I don't know. It's actually kind of cute." Trent admitted, handing each of them a glass. Jacen shook his head but took the glass and looked out of Trent's balcony to the Hudson River. In the night sky, the lights on the buildings radiated off of the moonlight.

"With this view, why'd you ever moved back to Boston?" Jacen heard Donovan say to Trent.

"I love Boston, period." Trent said, handing the last glass to Jacen's brothers.

"A toast, gentlemen." Trent began. "To the last man standing, as of tonight, welcome to the club." Cheers went around as they all threw the shot back.

"So, what do you have planned, Trent?" Justin asked.

"Nothing that will get us arrested." He stated plainly.

"I would hope not." Jerome answered. As a Boston Detective, Jerome pretty much walked the straight and narrow. Trent shrugged his shoulders, walked over to an ottoman, pulled open a drawer, and then closed it. He walked directly over to Jacen.

"Here put this on." Trent instructed. Jacen's brows hunched as he put his glass down and grabbed the item in Trent's hand.

"You have got to be kidding." Jacen said, realizing Trent handed him a blindfold.

"Not at all, my friend, and hurry up. The Party bus will be here shortly to pick us up." Jacen looked around as Donovan and his brothers all looked at him with a smirk. He shook his head.

"Just make sure I make it to my wedding in one piece." Jacen warned.

"Yeah, yeah, put the blindfold on." Trent hurried him. Jacen shook his head one more time and exhaled. He put the blindfold on and prayed he lived through the night.

~~~~~~~~~~~~~~~~~~~~~~~~~~~~~

Chelsea did her best not to cry as her soon-to-be mother-in-law pinned her 'something borrowed' on her dress, officially welcoming her into the family. She smiled and hugged her. Nancy and the other Turner wives, along with Erica and Kaitlyn, all exited the room, getting ready for the ceremony. Only Ashiree was left behind. Happier than she could ever be, Chelsea walked over to the wall-length mirror.

"Will you help me?" She asked Ashiree, needing to put on her veil and calm her nerves.

"Of course." she watched as her best friend appeared in the mirror behind her. Ashiree lightly placed the flowered tiara on her head. Chelsea sighed, remembering bits and pieces of their conversation last night.

"So, where are you heading now?" Chelsea asked.

"Houston. There's an upcoming pharmaceutical company that's offered me a position." Ashiree answered. The tone in Ashiree's voice worried Chelsea.

"Are you ever going to settle down, Ree?"

"Who knows." Ashiree said, shrugging her shoulders. Chelsea turned around and faced her best friend.

"I worry about you." she admitted.

"You can't worry about me. It's your wedding day." Ashiree teased.

"I'm serious." Chelsea said, taking Ashiree's hands in hers.

"So am I... I'm fine."

"You always say you'll be fine." Chelsea said with genuine concern in her voice.

"Then why are you worried?" Ashiree asked. Chelsea inhaled a deep breath before answering.

"Because you can't keep running forever. At some point, you have to plant roots somewhere." She knew it was a sticky subject with Ashiree. Growing up in the foster system prevented her from being comfortable in one spot for too long.

"Well, we all can't find our prince charming like you." she joked, and Chelsea knew it was her way of lighting the mood around them and trying to change the subject.

"At this point, I'd settle for a steady boyfriend." Chelsea joked back but released her friend's hand.

"Come on Chels, you know that's not me." she did, but it didn't help her concern.

"I know, and it makes me worry...are you happy, Ashiree?" Chelsea genuinely wanted to know.

"Of course, I am. My best friend gets to marry the love of her life today." Ashiree proclaimed like it was a public declaration. Chelsea smiled at her.

"True, and it's the only reason I'm letting this go...for now." she said with a slight warning. Ashiree smiled at her and walked over to grab her bouquet.

"Then let's get you hitched." she said proudly, and Chelsea couldn't help but laugh at Ashiree's poor portrayal of a southern drawl. A slight knock on the door caught their attention as Ashiree handed Chelsea her bouquet. Ashiree quickly went to the door and peeked through the crack before opening it to allow her father to step in.

"Bells really are ringing." he said with a slight croak in his throat. "You look as beautiful as your mother."

"Oh, daddy, please don't cry. We don't have time to fix my make-up."

"I'll try and hold it in." Frederick managed to say without a tear falling.

"Are we all ready?" she heard the wedding coordinator say. She hadn't noticed she'd walked in behind her father. Chelsea nodded. This was it. Ashiree fluffed her dress one last time, and her father pulled the veil from her tiara and covered her face.

~~~~~~~~~~~~~~~~~~~~~~~~~~~~~~~

Jacen stood outside the sanctuary anxiously waiting to go in. Guests were already taking their seats as the ceremony was soon to begin.

"How are you feeling?" Jacen heard the voice of his older brother Justin approaching.

"Readier than I thought I'd be." He admitted. Justin nodded as a slow smile appeared on his face.

"I know that feeling." Justin confirmed.

"I'm sorry, Justin." Jacen admitted. He hadn't realized until the very moment that he hadn't actually apologized.

"For what?" Justin asked with a deepened brow.

"For not understanding and causing problems between you and Alexia.

"That's water under the bridge now."

"I know. But you're a much better man than I am. I think I would have tried to kill me if I were you." Justin chuckled at Jacen's words.

"Honestly, the thought hadn't crossed my mind. I did think about shaking some sense into you, but truthfully, your reaction wasn't what bothered me." Jacen quirked a brow in confusion.

"What do you mean?"

"I needed Alexia to want us. Every relationship will have its trials, and something will always try to come between what we share. We only survive when we're together. When we decide to choose us over everything else. I could have taken the easy route and blamed you. But my main concern at that time, was if I was worth it to Alexia. Was I worth her fighting for?"

"I didn't make that decision easy for her." Jacen responded. He knew at the time family was everything to Alexia. She'd broken up with Justin, determined not to be the rift between him and Justin. Jacen had been too self-concerned back then to understand the damage he was doing to the both of them.

"You didn't, but it worked out for the best." Justin said. Jacen nodded and smiled, truly happy that things had worked.

"The last man standing is about to take the plunge." Justin and Jacen turned, hearing Trent's voice as Donovan and his two other brothers approached.

"Are you nervous?" James asked.

"No." Jacen answered honestly.

"Was it my imagination, or did Fredrick Stone enter the church?" Jerome asked.

"You didn't imagine it. I saw him too." Donovan admitted.

"Who would have guessed Chelsea was his daughter." Trent stated. Jacen half-listened as they continued to talk about Chelsea's parentage. The attendees were relatively low due to the Hollywood moguls' attendance. Fredrick pulled a few strings to keep his whereabouts under the radar for Chelsea's wedding, keeping it free from a media fiasco. Jacen knew he could trust his family and friends to be discreet.

"Jacen, if you're ready, you all can go in and take your places." The wedding coordinator interrupted Jacen's thoughts and the conversation going on with the guys. He nodded and walked into the statuary. The first people he saw were his parents, and he smiled, watching as his father handed his mother a tissue and she dabbed her eyes. The ceremony hadn't even started, and she was already crying. Jacen stood in his designated spot with Justin to his left and took a deep breath. It seemed like forever before the bridal party entered the sanctuary, and the moment Jacen saw Chelsea on the arm of her father, he was happy he'd taken a breath because she was utterly breathtaking. In a flash, the ceremony went by. The exchanging of vows, the planting of the rings, and saying 'I Do' blurred together, until Jacen heard magic words to seal Chelsea to him forever.

"You may now kiss the bride." The preacher said. Jacen promptly lifted Chelsea's veil and kissed his wife. She was officially his. Jacen enjoyed every inch of her mouth pressed against his. But a part of him wanted to beat on his chest in triumph. He felt Chelsea smile against his lips, and he pulled back, smiling down at her.

"I love you, Mr. Turner." She said, partly laughing, knowing how much he honestly didn't care to be called that. But now, at this moment, it was the best thing in the world.

"I love you too, Mrs. Turner."

~~~~~~~~~~~~~~~~~~~~~~~

"I know that look." Justin Turner Sr. said, leaning over to his wife as he gently placed a kiss on her cheek. Nancy Turner, affectionately known as 'Momma Turner', smiled, accepting the gentle kiss from her husband of more than forty years.

"What look is that?" She asked coyly.

"Pure Bliss." Justin said. She nodded. He was right. Turning her head back to the dance floor, her eldest sons were playing keep the bride away from her baby boy. Even now, at thirty-one years old, Jacen would always be her baby. She did her best today to not cry, but the moment she pinned something borrowed on Chelsea's dress, the water leaks started and didn't stop until after the ceremony. Laughing now at the quick maneuver Chelsea made on the dance floor into the arm of her best friend, Momma Turner smiled and laughed as her oldest sons teasingly complained of the bride not cooperating.

"How about I get you some more champagne?" Her husband suggested. She smiled, knowing he was heading over to grab himself a Jameson on the rocks. As he walked over to the bar area, she couldn't help but appreciate how handsome he was. Forty-plus years later and she was still attracted and very much in love with him. Turning her eyes back on the dance floor. She noticed Chelsea sitting on the side speaking with her friend Ashiree. Another very special young lady she hoped would find love if she ever settled down long enough. She watched a very determined Jacen cross over to where Chelsea and Ashiree sat and scooped Chelsea up in his arms, carrying her back onto the dance floor. The joy on her son's face melted her heart. He'd found his one. As they continued dancing, Nancy looked at her other sons, each standing beside their wives. She'd always wanted a daughter, but God had not seen fit to bless her with one; instead, He now blessed her with four. Catcalls and applause rang out in the room as Jacen now dipped his bride and kissed her. Others began to join the bride and groom on the dance floor as her husband returned with her drink. Accepting the drink as he sat, she thanked him and took a sip, shuttering a little as the bubbles tickled her nose. She heard Justin chuckle at her shudder and couldn't help but laugh also. Shifting her eyes back to the dance floor, she hunched a brow at an unfamiliar face. She knew practically everyone that was in attendance or at least had seen their faces before.

"Do you know who that is dancing with Ashiree?" She asked her husband.

"Yes, that's Donald's grandson, Dominic Blake."

Epilogue

Anastazia waved to her Uncle Jacen and Aunt Chelsea as she pulled away from the brownstone. Her phone chimed, and she noticed her mother was calling and answered through the Bluetooth in her car.

"Hello, mother."

"Stazia, sweety, where are you ?"

"I'm just leaving Uncle Jacen's house."

"Alright, your father, brother, and I are at your Uncle Jerome's house. Why don't you swing by?"

"Okay, I'll swing by. Should I stop and get anything?" Anastazia knew that if they were over at her Uncle Jerome's place, he was most likely throwing some meat on the grill.

"Shayna says no, we have everything. Oh wait, your brother would like you to stop by the store and get him some takkis." Anastazia almost rolled her eyes. She loved her brother, but she swore he would turn into a takki if he ate another bag.

"Okay, I'll be there shortly." She responded then disconnected the call.

Twenty minutes later, she parked in the driveway of her other uncle's home behind her parents' black SUV. Exiting her vehicle and grabbing her brother's snack from the back seat, she headed to the front door. Deciding not to bother with knocking, she opened it instantly, hearing her mother and Aunt Shayna talking in the kitchen.

"Knock, knock, I'm here." she announced, walking into the kitchen.

"Stazia, hi sweetie." Her aunt Shayna exclaimed, abandoning the salad bowl she was just using.

"Hi, auntie Shayna." she said, happily accepting the hug she knew was coming.

"I can't believe the little woman you're growing up to be." Her aunt said.

"You say that every time." Anastazia said smiling.

"Did you get my takkis?" Her brother said, practically running up to her.

"Hello, Jay Jay." she said. He rolled his eyes and went to reach for the bag in her hand. She quickly swept it away from him, holding the bag over her head so he couldn't reach it.

"Mom!!" he complained.

"Jay Jay, say hello to your sister."

"But I just saw her this morning." He complained. Anastazia watched as her mother gave her brother a very stern look. He sighed and exhaled.

"Hi Anastazia." he said gruffly.

"Here you are." she said, handing the bag to him. He snatched it and stuck his tongue out, and then ran out of the kitchen.

"Boys!" she said and turned back to her mother and aunt. "So what's the special occasion? Uncle Rome rarely grills." her mother and aunt nodded and chuckled, but before they could answer, someone else entered the kitchen.

"I guess the special occasion is me." Anastazia turned her head slowly at the deep sensual voice that had spoken. Her eyes connected with light brown ones, encompassed in a beautiful chocolate brown face. Full lips with the hint of a growing mustache and a cleft chin.

"Clifton?" she said, trying to get her bearings, knowing both her aunt and mother were present. What happened to the little boy she'd grown up with?

"It's good to see you, Staz." Clifton said, walking over and engulfing her in a hug. She did her best not to breathe in his musky scent and minty breath.

"It's good to see you too." she said, taking a step back and feeling slightly flustered. "What are you doing here?" she asked. She hadn't seen Clifton in almost three years. His mother moved away from Boston when Clifton's father was killed. Clifton had been five years old at the time and had visited with Jerome and Shayna ever so often over the years.

"I'm here for the summer." he said with a shrug.

"And has been a pain in my butt since he got here." her cousin Miracle stated as she joined them in the kitchen.

"Miracle, be nice. Clifton is family." Shayna warned.

"I know, mom. He's like the annoying older brother I never wanted." Miracle responded while playfully bumping Clifton's side. He smiled down at Miracle's teasing, and Anastazia had to focus on steadily breathing.

"Anastazia, are you alright?" her mother asked. She shot her head over to her mother, praying she hadn't read her thoughts.

"It's just a little hot in here." she quickly stated.

"Oh, you girls, get out of here. The oven is on for the macaroni in cheese." Shayna explained.

"That sounds delicious." Clifton said.

"Come on, Stazia, let's go up to my room." Miracle suggested while grabbing her hand and practically dragging her out of the kitchen.

"It was good to see you, Staz. Maybe we'll get to hang out sometime." Clifton called out before she was completely out of the kitchen.

"Sure, I'd like that, Clifton." she said with a shaken breath. He winked, and her pulse went up a few notches. After entering Miracle's room, Anastazia sat on Miracle's bed trying to listen to her cousin's latest update on beauty tips from YouTube subscriptions she followed. But all she could do was play over and over in her head, seeing Clifton in the kitchen and wonder...What did that wink mean?

Made in the USA
Middletown, DE
29 August 2021

46829285R00159